The Widows of Westram

Widowed by war...tempted by new flirtations!

Lady Carrie and her sisters-in-law, Lady Petra and Lady Marguerite, each tragically widowed on the same day by the same battle in Portugal, have had time to come to terms with their circumstances.

Now these three beguiling widows aim to seize the day and build their own destinies—in life, and in the realm of romantic liaisons...!

Find out what happens in Marguerite's story:

A Family for the Widowed Governess

And read the other stories in
The Widows of Westram trilogy!

A Lord for the Wallflower Widow
An Earl for the Shy Widow

Author Note

I hope you enjoy this final story in The Widows of Westram series as much as I enjoyed writing it. It is always difficult to say goodbye to characters who feel like they have become friends during the journey to their happy ending, isn't it? I certainly feel that way with these three very different ladies. I am not sure where the idea of three widows whose husbands all died on the same day in the same place came from, but I had fun with it. I do love hearing from readers, be it a request for a story about a secondary character in an earlier book or for a chat about the story you are reading now. You can always reach me through my website, annlethbridge.com, or at Facebook.com/AnnLethbridgeAuthor or join the whole Harlequin Historical author team for fun and prizes at Facebook.com/HarlequinHistorical.

ANN LETHBRIDGE

A Family for the Widowed Governess

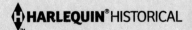

HARLEQUIN® HISTORICAL

Recycling programs
for this product may
not exist in your area.

ISBN-13: 978-1-335-63534-1

A Family for the Widowed Governess

Printed in U.S.A.

In her youth, award-winning author **Ann Lethbridge** reimagined the Regency romances she read—and now she loves writing her own. Now living in Canada, Ann visits Britain every year, where family members understand—or so they say—her need to poke around every antiquity within a hundred miles. Learn more about Ann or contact her at annlethbridge.com. She loves hearing from readers.

Books by Ann Lethbridge

Harlequin Historical

It Happened One Christmas
"Wallflower, Widow...Wife!"
Secrets of the Marriage Bed
Rescued by the Earl's Vows

The Widows of Westram

A Lord for the Wallflower Widow
An Earl for the Shy Widow
A Family for the Widowed Governess

The Society of Wicked Gentlemen

An Innocent Maid for the Duke

Visit the Author Profile page
at Harlequin.com for more titles.

This story was about three women who became friends and supported each other through thick and thin. I would like to dedicate this book to great friends everywhere. These are people who make each day feel a little brighter and who are there for you in times of need as well as times of celebration. Friends are like treasure.
Hoard every one of them.

Chapter One

Lady Marguerite hated the way the ground sank and the water oozed up. A smell of wet mud filled her nostrils. It had taken her all morning to find the right ground conditions for the specimen she needed and she wasn't going to give up now, even if it did mean getting wet feet.

She slogged on across the meadow, stepping on the highest tussocks. At least, for the first time in a week, it wasn't raining. Indeed, it was a lovely spring day. Or it would be if she hadn't had to go specimen hunting in the boggy ground of a water meadow.

There! Finally. The yellow flower she was seeking. *Caltha palustris.* Or marsh marigold, as she had known it as a child. She picked her way over to the tall plant, aware that the water level here was higher than ever. Now each step created deep puddles that threatened her jean half-boots.

Ugh. She hated this part of her work. Gathering plants in the wild. Petra would have adored it, but

Petra was married and gone. The gentleman paying Marguerite to draw plants for his book was supposed to provide her with the specimens, but he'd said they were more prolific in Kent than where he lived and asked her to find one for herself.

She had thought it would be easy. She had seen them everywhere last spring. Unfortunately, she needed one in flower and very few were in bloom yet.

She tugged on the stalk. After a slight resistance, it pulled free of the muddy earth. She inspected it from root to tip. There were more plants, closer to the stream. Should she try for one with more flowers? This one had only two blossoms and one bud.

'Ouch!' A high-pitched scream rang out across the field.

Marguerite glanced wildly around. More screams. A child, she thought. At the edge of the field. She picked up her skirts and headed in the direction of the sound.

'Ooh! Ooh! It hurts. Ouch. Ouch.'

Was someone striking a little girl?

She flung her sample aside and ran, ignoring the water soaking through her boots. Then she saw two little girls, the bigger of them dancing around flapping her hands and making the sounds Marguerite had heard. There was no sign of any menacing presence. Marguerite rushed up to the one who was clearly in pain.

'What is it?'

'Ouch. Ouch.' Tears were running down the

child's face. 'I was picking flowers and something bit me.'

The younger child came over to stand beside her... sister? They looked alike. Brown hair. Big brown eyes and dressed exactly the same. Where on earth had they come from?

Marguerite grabbed one of the flapping hands and inspected it. Raised bumps with scarlet edges. She knew exactly what had happened. She cast her gaze around until she found what she wanted. Dock leaves. She scrunched up a couple to free their juices, then began rubbing them all over the little girl's hands.

After a few moments, the little girl's cries subsided to a whimper and she gazed up at Marguerite, her face sad. 'Why did the flower bite me?' She pointed to a little blue cornflower.

Marguerite winced. 'It didn't. It is hiding in a bed of stinging nettles. Those tall green plants. That is what hurt you.'

'Stinging nettles?' She kicked out at the plant.

Marguerite pulled her back. 'Careful. They can easily sting through your stockings.' Hadn't every child in England learned that the hard way?

The younger child crouched down and peered at the nearest nettle. 'Nasty flower,' she said.

Marguerite inspected the older child's hand. It was still swollen and sore looking. She rubbed some more. 'You put your hand right into the middle of them.'

The child gazed at her sadly, tears staining her little face. 'Why do they sting?'

'To stop you from picking them. Or rather, to stop grazing animals from eating them. It is the way the plant protects itself.'

The little girl pulled her hand from Marguerite's and inspected the damage. 'It still hurts. And I wasn't going to pick it. I was picking the blue one.'

'It will hurt for a while, I am afraid. And itch.' She picked more dock leaves. 'Keep rubbing the sore places with this until it goes away.'

She glanced around. They were a good mile from Ightham village and even further from her home in Westram. 'Where do you live?'

The smaller child pointed away from Ightham. 'Over there. In a big house.' She spread her arms to aid in her description.

Marguerite knew of only one big house in this particular area, though she had never visited it. Good lord. Marguerite had assumed they were children of villagers, or tenants, but now that she had time to look more closely, she could see that their dresses and pinafores were of far too good a quality to be worn by children of common folk. 'You mean Bedwell Hall. You are Lord Compton's daughters?'

The older girl left off sucking the back of her hand and nodded.

Marguerite recalled her abandoned specimen with a sigh. She'd have to pick one another day, because these children should not be wandering around in the fields alone. What on earth could Lord Compton be thinking?

'Come along, ladies. It is time you went home.'

The younger one giggled. 'Ladies.'

'You are ladies, are you not?' Marguerite said.

The older one left off her rubbing. 'I am Lady Elizabeth and she is Lady Jane. Everyone calls me Lizzie.'

'I'm Janey,' the younger one added.

Marguerite took their hands. How tiny they were. And grubby. It made her think of her childhood. When she had been young and innocent. She could scarcely remember it. Mama had died when she was very young and then it seemed as if she had become mother to her siblings, especially to her sister, Petra.

And now Petra had remarried, leaving Marguerite entirely alone. She liked it that way. She really did. Not having to care for anyone else, being able to do exactly as she pleased, when she pleased, was heaven. And if she needed company, she could always call on Petra and her new husband, Ethan, or go for a visit to Carrie and Avery at their home in the north of England.

Right now, Petra and her husband were off visiting Ethan's elderly relative in Bath. Ethan had thought Petra was looking a little peaky and had thought a change of air would do her good. Bless the man. He really was good to her younger sister.

They climbed a stile and crossed a narrow laneway bounded by a high wall.

'The gate is that way,' Lizzie said.

They really were quite a distance from the house. It did not seem right at all. 'How old are you, Lizzie?'

'I am eight,' Lizzie said, 'and Janey is six.'

Marguerite frowned. 'Are you supposed to be wandering around the fields on your own?'

'No,' Lizzie said. 'But we ran away.'

A cold chill travelled down Marguerite's spine. 'Why?'

'Because Papa is mean to us,' Janey said. 'So we runned away.'

'Ran,' Marguerite said. She did not like the sound of this. Not at all. How many times had she, too, had the urge to run away?

In the end, it had been Neville who left her. She never had understood why he, of all people, had gone off to war with her brother and brother-in-law, but of the three of the women left behind to become widows, she must have been the only one who celebrated her husband's departure with a toast to whatever impulse had sent him off.

She hadn't wanted his death. But she had been glad to see him go. Unfortunately, she wasn't yet free of the misery he had imposed on her life from the moment they wed. But she would be. Very soon.

Not far down the lane, a side gate into the Bedwell estate stood ajar.

She frowned at it. This lord did not care very much for the welfare of his children, that much was certain. She ushered the children through and closed it behind them, making sure it was firmly latched. With growing anger for this careless papa, she marched the two girls up the path to the back of a beautiful Palladian mansion. Once, this house had belonged to the Westrams. Back before Oliver Cromwell had turned England upside down.

It would not have looked like this then. It had been vastly improved since its Tudor days.

Not a soul hustled out to meet them. Had no one realised these girls were missing?

'My lord?'

Jack Vincent, Earl Compton, glanced up from reviewing his bailiff's weekly report on several matters relating to the estate. He frowned. Johnson was staring out of the estate office window with a puzzled expression.

'What is it?'

'A young woman, my lord. With Lady Elizabeth and Lady Jane in tow.'

Jack shot out of his chair and around the desk to see what Johnson was talking about. Indeed. It was as his bailiff had said. A willowy woman was striding across the stable yard with his daughters dragging their feet as she urged them along.

'Wait here,' he commanded. He strode for the kitchen door.

Cook looked up, flustered at his entry. 'Is there...?'

He opened the door to the courtyard and emerged into the spring sunshine. He blinked against the glare.

'Lord Compton?' an imperious, slightly out-of-breath voice asked.

He bowed slightly to the dishevelled woman whose hems were damp and muddy and who had locks of auburn hair dangling from beneath her cap as if she had been pulled through a hedge backwards. 'Who the devil are you? And what are you doing with my daughters?'

She recoiled and drew herself up straight. 'We have not met, but I am Lady Marguerite Saxby. I live in Westram.' Her mouth tightened. 'As for your other question, I found these ladies wandering in the field outside your walls. Lady Elizabeth has had an unfortunate encounter with a stinging nettle.'

He froze, looked at the tears staining his eldest child's face and felt anger rising inside him. How had this happened? 'Why were you outside?'

Lizzie flinched.

Damn it. He hated when she did that. He reached for a modicum of calm.

'We runned away,' Janey announced.

'Ran.' He and this woman, this Lady Marguerite, spoke at the same time.

He glanced at her. She glared back. As if *he* was somehow in the wrong.

'You know you are not allowed to go outside without a maid.' He sounded gruffer than he intended.

Lizzie lifted her shoulders. 'Nanny said everyone was busy.'

'Then you wait.' He ran his hands through his hair. 'Look, if you can't do as you are told, Lizzie, then I'm sorry, but you know the consequences.'

Lizzie burst into tears. 'Nooooo!'

The woman thrust herself between Lizzie and himself. 'Leave the poor child alone. She has been punished enough, I should think. Look.' She gently pulled Lizzie forward and held out her hand for his inspection.

It was covered in white bumps with red edges. His stomach churned. His brain went numb at the sight of the painful swelling. 'Go,' he yelled. 'Upstairs. Get Nanny to put something on it.'

'I gave her dock leaves,' Lady Marguerite said. Her voice was beautifully modulated, if a little deeper than most women's. For some reason it calmed him.

She crouched down. 'Take the leaves to your nanny, she will know what to do.' Lizzie nodded and ran off with Janey scurrying behind.

Jack hated to see his children hurt. Could not abide it. Why the devil would they not do as he had instructed and stay indoors with Nanny James?

The young woman rose to her feet. She was almost tall enough to look him in the eye. And delightfully feminine, despite her drab clothing. 'What on earth are you about, Lord Compton?'

He stared blankly 'About?'

'Those children should not be wandering the countryside alone. Anything could happen.'

'Do you think I don't know that?'

She blinked.

Damn and blast, he had raised his voice. Again. He lowered his tone. 'They know better. I have told them time and time again.'

Her finely arched eyebrows, a darker auburn than

her hair, lowered. Her pretty green eyes narrowed. 'The gate to the lane was open. They were a long way from home and you had no idea of it. Children of their age need proper adult supervision.'

Good lord, who was she to come here laying down the law? He was the magistrate. 'Nonsense. They have proper supervision. Indoors.'

'I see.' She looked completely unconvinced.

'There is a nanny, three footmen and a cook, all there to see that they have whatever their little hearts desire. Is that enough supervision for you, madam?' Devil take it, why was he explaining himself to this woman? He took a deep breath.

Somehow, she managed to look down her nose at him. 'Not enough of the right sort of supervision, apparently, and while a punishment is likely in order, I beg that it be denial of some privilege, a story at bedtime, a visit to the village, something that will not cause physical pain.'

Stunned, he stared at her. Pain?

She narrowed her eyes. 'Good day, Lord Compton.' She spun around and marched back the way she had come.

How dare she come here and accuse him of not looking after his children? And…and did she think he was going to beat them? Damn her, for judging him so poorly. 'Johnson, get a chain and a lock and secure the damned gate. And find out who left it open.'

He strode for the nursery. As he expected, his daughters, his little girls, were gathered around

Nanny's chair. They looked so innocent. So sweet. They were the bane of his life.

No. No. That was not true. But somewhere along the line he had lost control. And that would not do. A man needed to be in control of his family or bad things happened. A shudder ran down his spine. The memory of what had happened to his wife when she took it in her head to go visit her scallywag of a brother without his knowledge leapt to the forefront of his mind. If he had been stricter, more in control of his wife, she would be alive today.

'Elizabeth, what on earth were you thinking?' He fixed his gaze on his oldest daughter. 'I have warned you about this sort of thing. This was your last chance, I am afraid. As I said, you must face the consequences.'

'Now, now, Master Jack,' Nanny said. 'What has you in a pelter?'

'In a *pelter*?' He stared at the woman who had been his wife's nanny. 'I can assure you I am not in a pelter. I would simply like to be informed why my daughters ignored my orders and went roaming the countryside. That is not too much to ask, is it?'

Elizabeth stared at the carpet and the toe of her shoe traced the pattern on the carpet. 'No, Papa,' she whispered.

Now he felt like an ogre. He steeled his resolve. He could not give in. Would not.

'We wanted to find a frog,' Janey announced as if that was a perfectly good explanation. 'Bert told

Sam there are frogs in that field over there. He put one in his sister's bed and made her scream.'

She was talking about two of his grooms. Which meant they had been hanging about the stables. Another thing they were not supposed to do. Horses were dangerous.

Janey's eyes filled with tears. 'But we couldn't catch one. Then I wanted to pick a bouquet for you, but I couldn't reach the flower and then the weeds bit Lizzie and she screamed. I was frightened.'

He winced. 'Were you?'

She nodded. 'Then the nice lady came along.' She beamed up at him. 'And here we are.' Her expression changed. 'We didn't mean to be bad, Papa. It won't happen again.' Her lower lip trembled. He reached out and she stepped into the circle of his arm.

'No crying,' he said. He couldn't bear it if they cried. He picked her up and held her close to his chest. Unfortunately, they knew their tears troubled him and he was never sure if they were real or if they were simply using them to get their way.

He also did not fancy carrying out his threat. But how could he run his estate if he was always worrying about his girls getting into some sort of scrape? His only option was to send for his spinster aunt Ermintrude. She would keep the girls in order.

He'd been terrified of her as a lad. 'I am sorry, but I cannot have the rules disregarded in this way. I will write to your great-aunt today.'

Nanny paled. 'They won't do it again, dearie.'

Netty climbed on to Nanny's lap and stuck her

thumb in her mouth. Almost three already. He could scarcely believe it was nearly two years since Amanda had been brutally murdered. And still Netty wasn't talking. Nanny kept telling him there was nothing wrong. That she would talk when she was ready, but Jack was starting to worry.

'Please, Papa,' Elizabeth said, clasping her little hands to her chest. 'We promise we won't do it again.'

No tears from Elizabeth.

'You promise?' he said, suddenly weary. 'On your word of honour?'

'Yes. I promise. Cross my heart and hope to die.'

He put Janey down. 'This really is your very last chance.'

'Yes, Papa,' the girls chorused.

Exhaustion rose in him. 'Very well. But I am holding you to your promise. A Vincent always keep his or her word.'

They hung their heads. 'Yes, Papa.'

Nanny cocked her head on one side. 'You did thank the lady, my lord? For bringing the girls home?'

Had he? All he recalled was trying to defend himself from her unwarranted attacks on his character. Damn, no doubt he'd been rude. He usually was these days. He didn't have time for niceties and walking around on eggshells. 'I will thank her next time I see her. And I will see you both at bedtime.'

He left before they convinced him to do something else that was against his better judgement.

Frogs indeed. Apologies to rude young women. Yet another chance. Was he losing his grip on things?

He pitied the men who married his daughters. They wouldn't stand a chance.

Not that he had any intention of letting any man within a hundred miles of them before they were at least twenty-five.

Perhaps he should try another governess. The girls had chased two off already. He needed one with a strong character.

Two days later, and after another foray into a bog closer to home, Marguerite could not get the sight of those dejected little girls out of her mind. Nor the way their father loomed over them. He'd been terrifying. Dark haired, broad shouldered, tall and ruggedly handsome. Handsome? Well and so he might be, but looks meant nothing. It was actions. He was clearly a brute.

She had wanted to say more on the matter of punishment, but she also knew that sometimes arguing with angry males only made them worse. She could only hope that he had calmed down before he decided on a punishment. He had seemed to listen to her words, even if he had seemed shocked by her temerity at speaking up.

She had quickly learned not to argue with Neville or he would find some way to hurt her: a pinch on her arm, a slap to the back of her head, places where no one would see the marks. But Neville was gone and she was dashed if she would remain silent while another man did things she did not like.

Marguerite stared at the dissected flower on the table. She needed to stop thinking about the broodingly handsome Lord Compton and his children and concentrate on drawing this plant. She only had this one to complete and she would have completed her contract and she could send them away. If all was approved, she should get her payment within two weeks.

Lord knew she needed it.

Instead of worrying about those two little girls she should be worrying about what was in the pantry for dinner. But that would have to come later, when she had finished this sketch. She picked up her ruler and measured each yellow petal.

When next she raised her gaze, she realised what had been troubling her for the past half-hour. She rubbed her eyes. It was almost too dark to see. With the light rapidly fading, she would have to finish the work tomorrow. She got up, stretched and lit two candles. Not enough to work by, but enough that she would not fall over the furniture.

She went down to the kitchen. Bread and cheese would have to do for this evening.

A scrap of paper sticking out from beneath her door caught her eye. Her stomach fell away. It could not be… He had given her a month to get the money together. She snatched up the paper and took it over to the table, where the light was better.

Five pounds. A week hence. To be deducted from the final payment.

She dropped her head in her hands. How on earth could she get five pounds in a week? She would have to meet him and explain.

Oh, what an idiot she had been to draw that picture. A thirteen-year-old idiot who had had the mad idea she would become famous and admired for her talent. Famous artist? What a joke. Yes, she was good at copying things exactly, but it had come as a rude awakening when she had discovered she did not have the skill required to bring her paintings to life. Technically good, the drawing master had said, but no flair. Peeved by the comments, she had launched herself into a furious caricature of her teacher. Her brothers and sister roared with laughter at her depiction. Encouraged, she had drawn their neighbours and friends, highlighting their foibles with what she thought was wit. Her siblings' laughter and admiration had been heady, but, as they say, pride went before a fall. Drawing a very unflattering and lewd picture of the Prince of Wales with his mistress was the worst mistake she had ever made. What an idiot she had been to sign that dreadful sketch.

But hers wasn't the only blame. Even she'd had the sense not to show anyone that particular sketch. She should have burned it. Of course, Neville, when he found it, had to show his horrid friends. Embarrassment rose in her in a hot, horrible tide. They had all seen it and laughed about it like nasty little boys. But once the novelty wore off, she'd been sure he'd destroyed it. He'd said so. She swallowed bile. Trusting anything he said had been the height of stupidity.

If it did get published with her name on it, her family would be so ashamed. And if they tried to support her, they would likely also be ostracised from society. She could not let that happen. She had to get it back and destroy it. And since she didn't know the identity of the man who had approached her at Petra's wedding and had no way to contact him, she would just have to find a way to get the money. She had begged him to wait until she could gather enough money to pay him what he was asking. Twenty-five pounds was a fortune, but with her next payment from the publisher, and using the money she had saved for next quarter's rent, she could do it.

She bit her lip. Perhaps she should ask her brother Red, the Earl of Westram, for money, but knowing Red he would insist on knowing why she needed it and likely insist she live with him. Unfortunately, he was about to marry a woman who she really did not like. She had no trouble imagining how miserable she would be under that woman's thumb. It would be nearly as bad as being married to Neville. Red's future wife did not approve of independent women. Or artists. Or life in general. How on earth could Red—?

She cut the thought off. He had offered for Miss Featherstone and she had accepted and that was all there was to it. But one thing was certain: Marguerite was not going to move into their home.

If only Petra and Ethan were not away at the moment. She might have gone to them for a loan. Petra would give her whatever she needed. But then again, if Marguerite started to borrow money, where would it end? No. She had insisted on her independence and she was determined to make her own way. It just seemed so unfair that Neville had come back from the grave to ruin everything.

Her head started to ache.

She winced. That was all she needed. A headache. She put the kettle on to boil. A tisane would help and a little willow bark. And then she would figure out a way to earn some extra money.

Chapter Two

Jack had indeed been rude to Lady Marguerite Saxby. Marguerite. What a pretty name. Every time he spotted daisies in his lawn or on the roadside, which was all the time, he was reminded that he owed her an apology. Which was why, two days after she had brought his girls home, he was here in Westram village, wondering how to visit her in a way that would not get tongues wagging. It would be ideal if he came across her shopping in the village, or even picking flowers in her garden. A chance meeting would allow him to offer his gratitude and move on.

The post office seemed the best place to start his search. Once he'd had a chance to think about things clearly, he'd recalled who she was. He'd come across her name when he'd been called upon to help sort out the local vicar's wife. For some reason, she had taken to stealing from the villagers and blaming it on a band of gypsies camped nearby. While he had not met Lord Westram's widowed sisters during the course of his investigation, he'd certainly heard about them.

All three of them had been widowed on the same day. Their husbands had died on the Iberian Peninsula, having gone off together to join the army because of some sort of wager. It had been quite the *on dit* among the *ton*. So much so, the story had made its way to his little corner of Kent.

No doubt Lady Marguerite would have learned about his wife's murder two years before. There had even been some who thought he might have done it, despite he had witnesses to account for his whereabouts. Perhaps that accounted for her hostility towards him.

'Good day, Lord Compton,' Mr Barker said. 'We don't often see you here in Westram.' His beady eyes were alight with curiosity. Devil take the man.

'I was passing through and recalled I was in need of...' his gaze fell on a stone jar behind the counter '...snuff.'

Barker looked shocked. 'My lord, I do not think that what I have is in any way up to your refined taste.'

In other words, why on earth would a man of his stature want to buy cheap snuff? 'Oh, 'tis not for me, but for my children's nanny.'

Barker instantly cheered. He took down the jar and began weighing. 'An ounce is enough, my lord?'

'Perfect,' Jack said. The noticeboard caught his eyes, or rather a very artfully drawn poster. *Drawing teacher willing to provide lessons*, it proclaimed.

'Notice went up yesterday,' Barker said. 'Lady

### Ann Lethbridge 27

Marguerite, looking for students.' He shook his head in a 'what is the world coming to' sort of way.

How very…fortuitous. 'I see.' He tipped his head as if considering the matter. 'My daughters could benefit from some drawing lessons. The older one has some talent, I think.'

'Lady Marguerite would be the right sort of person for your daughters, my lord. Very nice in her taste, she is. You'll find her at Westram Cottage, should you wish to enquire.'

He could not have found a better excuse to visit the widowed Lady Marguerite. He nodded. 'Thank you, Barker. How much do I owe you for the snuff?' He paid with the coin he had in his pocket and left the shop with a more purposeful step than when he had entered.

Westram Cottage lay at the far end of the village. A pretty little place, with yellow roses growing in the garden and over a trellis around the front door.

Did he really want to give in to this unusual impulse to hire a drawing teacher?

What he really needed was a governess for his daughters. She would teach them drawing. So, was this about his daughters, or about his interest in the lady? Because he could not seem to get her out of his head.

Nonsense. Nanny was right. He owed her an apology. The fact that she was looking for paid employment was also a puzzle. A widow living alone was usually of independent means. Now, puzzles interested him. He liked solving mysteries. Therefore, it was not the lady herself that had him intrigued, but her circumstances. For example, what had she been doing tramping around the countryside by herself? And looking delightfully dishevelled to boot?

He pushed that thought away. Nanny James was right, he really did owe her a thank-you.

He knocked on the door. Silence. No footsteps coming to the door. No sounds of occupation coming from inside. He stepped back and looked up. No smoke coming from any of the chimneys either. Clearly the lady was not home. Nor were any of her servants.

He pulled his card from his pocket, intending to write a promise to call on her the next day, when he heard a scraping sound from the rear of the house. Likely a groom working in the stables. Someone he could ask about the lady's whereabouts and expected hour of return. He followed the path around the side of the house to a small stable at the end of a well-cared-for garden.

He entered the stable and gaped at the sight of Lady Marguerite, mucking out in a pair of men's breeches and boots. He should leave.

Too late! As if sensing his presence, the woman looked up, pushed a lock of hair behind her ear and gaped back at him. 'Lord Compton,' she said. She glanced down at herself and winced.

She straightened, holding her shovel before her like a shield. It did nothing to hide her lovely figure. 'To what do I owe the pleasure?'

Devil take it. The woman must be one of those freethinking sorts. No wonder she had seemed so odd the day before. Was she really the sort of person he wanted teaching his girls?

'I…er…' He still held his calling card in his hand. He held it out.

She made no move to take it.

He cast around wildly for something to say and decided, as usual, that the truth was best. 'I apologise for my interruption. Having received no answer at the front door and hearing sounds of activity, I came to enquire when you might be expected home.'

She frowned. 'I see.'

'I came to apologise for my rudeness. I should have thanked you for bringing my daughters safely home. My concern overrode my good manners, I am sorry to say. So…thank you.'

She leaned her shovel against the stable wall and folded her arms. 'Apology accepted.'

He did not feel as if it was accepted. It seemed to be more a question of it being tolerated as being due, but not particularly welcome.

'I saw your notice in the post office,' he said.

'Oh?' Again, she swept back that unruly curl. The rest of her hair was severely restrained beneath her plain widow's cap. 'Were you interested in drawing lessons for your daughters?'

Hah. Finally, he had caught her interest. Why he might have wanted to see the sharpening of her gaze, and the curiosity in her expression, he could not imagine. And now what was he to say? No? 'I was interested in discussing the matter, certainly.'

'I see.'

Good lord, the woman was positively enigmatic with her answers. In his experience, most women were garrulous in the extreme and said little of import. This one seemed to put a world of meaning into every syllable.

'When might you be available to discuss the matter?' he said firmly, determined to take charge of this one-sided conversation. 'Shall I call on you tomorrow?' When he returned he would tell her he had changed his mind. She was not the sort of influence he wanted for his children.

She waved an arm. 'Now is as good a time as any.'

Blast.

She upturned a bucket and perched on it. He leaned against one of the posts supporting the rails of the nearest stall. There was only one equine occupant. A small grey mare with a dark circle around one eye. The animal looked well fed and well cared for.

'Where is your groom?' he asked, unable to contain his question any longer.

She started. 'Um… He is not here at the moment. He has gone to visit his sick mother.'

Jack narrowed his eyes on her face. Her gaze did not meet his. He knew a lie when he heard one. He'd become an expert, both at home and with his work for the Parish. 'It would have saved us both embarrassment if someone had answered the front door,' he said, sounding more irritated that he intended.

She raised her chin. 'The servants have the day off.'

Another lie. He hated lies and deceit, and this lady was not very good at either. He was sincerely doubting the wisdom of this visit. He was going to have to extricate himself from the situation as best he could.

'Are your daughters interested in learning to draw?' Lady Marguerite asked, clearly anxious to change the topic from the issue of her servants. For some reason, despite he didn't trust her to speak the truth, her worry troubled him.

With the exercise of a good deal of self-control, he avoided staring at the shapely legs encased in buckskin and neatly crossed at the ankle. 'I honestly do not know,' he said. 'I saw your advertisement quite by chance. I have not given it proper consideration.'

She sighed. There was something resigned about that sigh. It only added to his disquiet. Nevertheless, she straightened her spine and now looked him in the eye. 'My fee is one guinea per hour for both girls. I would suggest two hours of lessons two afternoons a week. At least, until they have mastered the rudiments. I require payment by the week in advance.'

Well, that was frank speaking. He narrowed his eyes. 'May I enquire as to your qualification for such instruction?'

She looked startled, then blushed, a beautiful wash of colour that rose from her neck to her forehead. He relaxed. The woman was nowhere near as controlled and detached as she made out.

* * *

Marguerite felt herself go hot all over and knew that her face would now be scarlet. She hated the way she blushed at the slightest thing. And it wasn't just because he was handsome and looking at her with an intensity that for some reason made her stomach flutter. This time it was justified. Blast it, she had been so taken with her idea about giving lessons, she hadn't given a thought to qualifications.

Or at least... 'I can show you some of my work,' she said. 'But I must be honest. While I took lessons as a girl in the schoolroom, I have never taught anyone.'

He pursed his lips. Such a stern, serious man. A tall man with broad shoulders. In the old days, when her brothers ran riot on their estate, they might have described him as a bruiser of a man. But he was more than that. He was a nobleman and he was a gentleman in his prime. A very attractive gentleman, for all that he seemed to view the world with suspicion.

He clearly hadn't liked apologising to her, or expressing his gratitude. And why on earth had he come around to the back of her house? Any rational gentleman would have simply written a note on his card, stuck it beneath the knocker and left. On the other hand, he was the local magistrate. Perhaps he made a habit of prowling around other people's property.

In the dim light of the stable, the way he stood looming over her, he looked almost menacing. As if he would arrest her and lock her up in a heartbeat, given the opportunity.

Dash it all. She had had enough of being intimidated by a man. She glared back.

And besides, now she had admitted she had no qualifications to teach his children, he would politely refuse to employ her and go, leaving her to her embarrassment at being found mucking out the stables in a pair of old buskin breeches she had found while she was looking in the attic for rags with which to clean the windows.

The next job on her list.

Dash it, she should be drawing, not undertaking menial tasks. But until she could pay for the return of her sketch, she could not afford to hire anyone to help with the chores.

'Very well,' he said.

She looked at him blankly.

'I will look at your work.'

Relief filled her. 'If you would give me a moment, I will bring some out.'

He gave her a considering look. 'Why don't we go inside? I will make us a cup of tea while you fetch down your portfolio.'

'Make tea?' she said, scarcely believing her ears.

'I used to do so all the time when I was at university. I am sure I have not forgotten the way of it.' He tipped his head on one side. 'By the time the kettle boils you will have had a chance to…er…freshen up.'

Her mouth dried. He meant her to change her clothes. Heat scorched her face. The man probably

thought her completely harum-scarum. Not at all
the right sort of teacher for his children. But if she
could convince him to hire her, it would make her
life so much easier.

'I will meet you in the kitchen in ten minutes,' she
said. She left the barn, back straight and head held
high, and tried not to imagine him watching her as
she marched into the house.

She was almost finished dressing when she heard
the kitchen door open and close. Was he leaving?
Had she taken too long? The sound of china rattling
set her mind to rest. He must have lingered in the
stable to give her time to prepare herself. She had
not expected such courtesy from such a dour man.

She glanced in the mirror and pinned a stray lock
under her cap. There. That would have to do. She ran
down the stairs and into the kitchen.

His Lordship was nowhere to be seen.

'Lord Compton?'

He emerged from the pantry. 'I found some biscuits,' he said and grinned. He looked so startlingly
handsome, she stared at him open-mouthed. She'd
been saving those biscuits for the next time the vicar
came to call. The new vicar was a very pleasant
young man. And single. Not that Marguerite had any
interest in single gentlemen. But he always looked as
if he needed a good meal and always wolfed down
her biscuits.

His smile faded. 'I am sorry, I should not have
gone poking around in your pantry.'

She let go a breath. 'No. It is perfectly all right. I am glad you found them. I like biscuits. They are shortbread, I believe. My favourite.' Stop. He'd think her a fool for gabbling on like this. Indeed, there was a very odd look on his face. Disapproval, she thought.

She gestured to the table, where cups and saucers and the steaming teapot awaited. 'Won't you sit down?' She set her portfolio away from the teacups and took her seat. He took a chair opposite. She poured the tea and they sipped at it and nibbled on shortbread. This batch had turned out even better than the last, but if she didn't make some money soon, she would not be able to afford the butter to make more.

'Let me see your drawings,' he said after a few moments. She appreciated his getting down to business right away. She was beginning to feel uncomfortable about inviting a gentleman to take tea in her kitchen. It felt far too intimate to be alone with such a very handsome gentleman. One whom she found more attractive that she would have believed possible. As a rule, she preferred to give handsome, charming gentlemen a wide berth. She certainly didn't want to start tongues wagging in the village. Fortunately, the kitchen was at the back of the house, so passing neighbours were unlikely to know of his presence. Except...

'Oh, my goodness. What did you do with your carriage?' Was it parked outside in the lane?

'I left my horse at the inn,' he said.

She let go a sigh of relief.

His mouth tightened. 'The pictures?'

She pulled the portfolio closer, undid the worn blue ribbon and spread out samples of her still-life drawings before him.

After a moment of perusal, he lifted his gaze to meet hers. 'These are excellent,' he said.

Not a connoisseur, then. 'They are accurate depictions of the countryside hereabouts.'

He looked puzzled.

'I am a technician, my lord. I replicate what I see. I do not bring any great flair to the work.'

He shook his head. 'If either of my daughters could be taught to draw nearly as well, I would be satisfied indeed.'

Relief flooded through her. 'I believe I have the skill to pass my knowledge along. I have not forgotten my own lessons.'

'I have to warn you that my daughters are not the easiest children to teach. They have driven off two governesses in the past year alone.'

She hesitated and saw disappointment enter his gaze. She steeled her spine. 'I will do the best I can, my lord.'

'That is all I can ask. I agree to your terms. I will expect you on Wednesday afternoon, if that is convenient, and again on Friday.'

'That is convenient, my lord.' Heat travelled through her body. 'My fee is payable in advance, you will recall.'

'When you arrive on Wednesday, your fee will await you.'

She would have liked some of it today, but beggars could not be choosers. She nodded her acceptance.

He picked up his hat and left.

Two governesses driven off. What had she let herself in for?

The following Wednesday, Jack paced his study. At any moment Lady Marguerite was supposed to arrive.

Why the hell had he hired the woman? She had lied to him. A few discreet enquiries and he had the truth of the matter. Initially, there had been three widows living at the cottage. Two of them had wed, leaving Lady Marguerite alone. There were no servants. The maid and manservant who had been employed at the cottage had married and gone elsewhere. The lady had not hired anyone to take their places.

So why lie?

Because he would have disapproved of her lack of servants? Why would she care what he thought?

Because she needed the money from the drawing lessons. What lady would advertise for employment if she wasn't desperate? Clearly, Lord Westram should take better care of his sister.

Hah. The wry amusement that thought engendered gave him pause. Of course she wouldn't go to her brother, since the woman obviously valued her independence. Not the sort of influence he wanted for his daughters. But there was no going back since he had already offered her the position, or at least he had offered to give her the opportunity to prove she could do the job. He had also sent over one of his stable lads to take care of her horse and keep an eye on her. It wasn't right that a lady should live completely alone, mucking out her own stables and carrying her own coal.

If indeed she had any coal.

There had been a good pile of logs at the back door, though. Hopefully, his lad would have the sense to split them when he ran out of work in the stables. Jack went to his desk, looked at the pile of paperwork and then went to the window. It was nearly two in the afternoon. She should be here at any moment. Unless she intended to be fashionably late.

But no. He smiled at the sight of the trap advancing up his drive at a steady clip. He went outside to greet her.

A groom ran out from the stables to take her horse and held it steady while he helped her down. She was dressed in the same dun-brown coat she had worn the day she brought his daughters home. And as on that occasion, her hair was neatly pinned beneath a plain cap and covered by a serviceable bonnet with the sprig of daisies on the brim a startling little nod to femininity.

'Good afternoon, Lord Compton,' she said coolly.

'Good afternoon, Lady Marguerite.'

She gave him a tight little smile. 'Where might I find my charges?'

'In the nursery. Come. I will show you the way.'

He had spent his own childhood in this nursery with his own nanny. She'd been a little livelier than Nanny James was now. Certainly spryer. But there was no one else he would trust as much as he trusted her to care for his children.

Sounds of excited talking and giggling grew louder as they walked along the corridor. He made his step extra heavy, the sound echoing off the walls. The sounds ceased. He threw open the door and the three children were lined up in a row opposite, just as he had requested the previous evening. As was her wont, Nanny James was sitting beside the hearth, rocking back and forth and smiling at the little row of children. He smiled at them. His children were a credit to him.

'Good afternoon, daughters,' he said.

'Good afternoon, Papa,' the older two chorused, showing off their best curtsies. Netty removed her thumb from her mouth with a little pop and wobbled when she bent her knees. He really should try to have Nanny break her of the habit of thumb-sucking. He just didn't have the heart. She was still barely more than a baby. And besides, as Nanny always said when he discussed the matter with her, how many adults did he know who walked around sucking their thumbs?

'Ladies, this is Lady Marguerite, whom you know already. She has kindly agreed to give you drawing lessons. You will behave and do exactly as she says.'

'Yes, Papa,' they said in unison.

He handed Lady Marguerite the paper he had prepared that morning. 'This is a list of rules with regard to the children's activities. Please ensure they are followed.'

Lady Marguerite took the list with raised eyebrows. 'I will let you know if I think they are suitable.'

He gritted his teeth. 'They are my rules.'

'I see.' She glanced around the nursery. 'We cannot work in here, I am afraid. The girls need tables, easels and drawing implements.'

He'd thought of that. 'Let me show you the schoolroom. I am sure you will find it meets your needs.'

He led her to the very end of the hallway and opened the door. 'Will this do?'

It was a large airy space that he and his wife had prepared for the large brood they had expected. They had incorporated it into this wing of the house with a good deal of joyful anticipation. Now it only made him feel sad.

Lady Marguerite nodded. 'This will do very well, my lord.'

'The cupboard contains supplies I obtained on the instructions of the last two governesses. I recall they included things like pens and ink and charcoal.'

She crossed to the cupboard and scanned its contents. He could not help but admire the way she strode across the room with a purposeful step. She was ladylike, but also confident as his wife had never been. Which was why he still did not understand why on earth she would have gone out when night was drawing in on foot and alone. A lie. To himself. He knew why. She had gone alone and without talking to him because she knew he would not approve.

'This looks like a very good start,' Lady Marguerite said and turned to face him.

'Excellent. Let me know if anything else is required.'

She glanced around. 'If we could have this table moved closer to the window, it would be better.'

'I'll send a man up to do it.'

She nodded and looked down at his note. She ran her eye down the list and frowned. 'This is very restrictive, my lord.'

'As you have seen already, the girls are not easy to manage. I believe these rules will ensure their safety.'

She took a little breath and he had the feeling she intended to argue with him about his instructions. Instead, she gave a little shake of her head. 'And my fee?'

He handed over four guineas. 'For this week. We will discuss the future on Friday.'

She slipped the money into her reticule. 'About the groom you sent to my house—'

'No need to thank me. I am simply ensuring you arrive on time to give your lessons.'

'But—'

'No buts. I do not want the smell of horses in my daughters' schoolroom.'

She glared at him and muttered something under her breath. It sounded a bit like 'Men. Impossible.'

He pretended not to hear. 'Shall we fetch Elizabeth and Janey?'

She pressed her lips in a straight line and for one long moment he thought she was going to refuse to teach them. Then her shoulders drooped a fraction and she nodded.

Damnation. He should be pleased, not feeling like a bully. He was right about needing to establish proper rules and regulations. He was the girls' papa. He could not risk anything happening to them. This was the best way to keep them safe.

Chapter Three

Marguerite showed the girls how to draw basic shapes—squares, circles, triangles and ovals—and set them to practising on slates. There was no sense in using up valuable paper for this exercise. Lizzie was reluctant, but eventually complied.

While the girls worked she stood behind them and, with one eye on what they were doing, she re-read His Lordship's list of rules.

The children were to remain in the schoolroom at all times. They were to be walked from the nursery and back again. Walked. No running allowed. They were to have a snack sent up after the first hour of lessons. They were not to go outside or downstairs. She was also to make sure they minded their manners and, if they were rude, she was to report them to Nanny or himself.

She frowned. Were their lives so completely regimented? The man seemed to want to control every aspect of what they did or did not do. A shiver ran down her spine. She had not grown up under such strict controls, but she had experienced it with her husband. It had been awful. Was Lord Compton like Neville? If so, could she actually be complicit in something she did not like or believe in?

'Is this right, my lady?' Janey asked.

She had drawn a lovely circle. One of the hardest things to master. The line wavered a bit here and there, but for a first try it was very good.

'That is exactly what is needed,' Marguerite said.

Janey put down her chalk and shook her hand. 'That was hard.'

'It is not easy,' Marguerite admitted. 'But it is worth the effort. Lizzie, how are you doing?'

The child sat back. She had copied all of the demonstrated shapes across her slate in a rather slapdash manner. The circle did not join up. The triangles lines overlapped. The square looked more like a diamond.

Marguerite smiled. 'A very good first attempt.' She drew a circle next to the one Lizzie had drawn. 'See if you can get it looking a bit more even. The lines are supposed to touch.'

'This is silly,' Lizzie said, folding her hands across her chest. 'I want to draw a picture. Not shapes.'

'You cannot draw anything unless you know how to draw these shapes and several others I will show you,' Marguerite said. 'Everything is made up of shapes.'

Lizzie frowned. 'I don't understand. I want to draw a horse. It is horse shaped.'

Marguerite smiled. 'Let us see, shall we?' She moved to an empty space on the blackboard and started to draw. She showed them how circles and ovals and rectangles worked together to create the basic shape of a horse. 'This is only the start,' she said, turning to face them. 'But this is why you need to know these shapes.'

Janey clapped her hands. 'It looks just like a horse.'

Lizzie frowned. 'That looks nothing like a real horse.'

'But it will eventually,' Marguerite said. She softened the lines, drew the mane and tail. 'The better you get at controlling shapes, the easier it will become.'

Lizzie looked unconvinced, but rubbed her slate clean and started again.

A knock at the door. Their snack had arrived. Apples and cheese and milk, and tea for her. Well, at least the girls were properly fed. The two girls tore into the apples and gobbled up the cheese.

Marguerite laughed. 'Slow down, ladies. Where are your manners?'

The girls stopped and stared at her. They continued to eat, but with much more decorum. Yet Marguerite had the feeling they were holding themselves back. As if they were starving. How could that be? Was it possible that they were deprived of food as some sort of punishment?

Once they had finished and cleaned up they went back to drawing on their slates.

* * *

By the end of the second hour, Marguerite had them connecting shapes.

'Very soon, you will be ready to start putting your drawings on paper,' she said as they cleared up the slates and chalks to put them away. 'If you want to practise these shapes by yourself, you may.'

'Oh, we are not allowed in here without a teacher,' Lizzie announced. 'And Papa is still looking for a governess for us.'

And when he found one, his need for her would be at an end. All governesses taught drawing along with the other necessary lessons a girl needed to prepare her for life. Indeed, drawing was the least important skill. Needlework, writing and reading were far more valuable.

'Who is teaching you lessons at the moment?'

'Nanny reads to us, when her eyes aren't too tired,' Janey said.

Marguerite frowned. This was not the way to bring up such spirited intelligent girls.

They walked back to the nursery. At the door, Lizzie turned and looked at her. 'Are you coming back tomorrow.'

'Not tomorrow, but the day after.'

Elizabeth gave her a narrow-eyed stare, as if she did not believe her.

Janey gave a little skip. 'Goody. I like drawing.' Lizzie ushered her into the nursery and then turned back. 'You don't have to come again if you don't want to. I am teaching Janey to read.' She went inside and shut the door.

What on earth did Lizzie mean? Since it had been a busy afternoon, with them learning lots of new things, Marguerite decided to ask her about it another time. She returned to the schoolroom for her outer raiment.

All afternoon, Jack had wanted to go up to the schoolroom to see how the girls were faring with their drawing teacher. He had personally overseen the snack to be taken up to them. What if the girls were misbehaving? What if Lady Marguerite was not following the rules? He had forced himself not to go and check. Until Lady Marguerite proved that she could not cope, he would leave her to it.

At precisely five minutes after four he went up to the schoolroom. The girls were not there and Lady Marguerite had her coat on and was putting on her bonnet.

'They are back with Nanny,' she said with a cool smile.

He frowned. 'Oh, I see. How did they get on? Did they behave themselves?'

She nodded. 'They did.'

That was a relief. He had threatened them with a fate worse than death if they did not behave like perfect little ladies with their new teacher. The odd thing was, the girls had never met Aunt Ermintrude. He had no idea why they had decided she was their worst nightmare. Perhaps it was his fault. He had threatened a visit from her often enough.

He stepped aside to allow Lady Marguerite to pass. 'I asked one of the lads to bring the trap around,' he said. 'It is waiting at the front door. I will see you here on Friday.'

She hesitated. Devil take it, was she not telling him the truth when she said the girls had behaved themselves? He hadn't seen any of the telltale signs that would indicate she was lying.

Lady Marguerite drew in a breath. 'Yes. I will be here on Friday at two in the afternoon and not a minute later.'

He winced. She must be referring to his rules about timeliness. Well, he simply wanted to make things clear, that was all. It was better if everyone knew where they stood.

'Allow me to escort you out.'

She shook her head. 'No need. I know my way.'

And with that she whisked by him and down the stairs.

He was damned if he was going to chase after her, no matter how much he might want to.

Later that evening, Marguerite waited anxiously in the designated spot, hoping to discover the identity of this man who was causing her such distress. Unfortunately, the alley running beside the Green Man led to a row of labourers' cottages behind it and it was hard to see anything at all since there was no moon this evening. This was not a good place to meet a man who offered nothing but threats.

Her heart thumped loudly in her chest. Her breathing sounded loud in her ears. She wanted to run.

The man who had sat in the pew behind her at Petra's wedding in St George's Church had been well-spoken and she *had* taken him for a gentleman. Now, she was beginning to doubt her judgement.

The sound of male laughter wafted from the inn as a door opened and spilled light into the alley. It closed, leaving the narrow lane seeming darker than ever. She swallowed.

The tap of footsteps on cobbles approached.

She held her breath.

'You have the money?' a cultured voice asked.

She could see only a silhouette in the gloom. 'I do.' She sounded a great deal calmer than she felt. A little spurt of pride gave her courage. She would not be intimidated or bullied by this man.

'Hand it over.'

She held out a knitted purse containing the guineas Lord Compton had given her and the few other coins she had scraped together to make up the sum he demanded. 'You have the sketch?'

The man plucked the purse from her hand. 'Not until I have payment in full.'

Disappointed, but not surprised, she grimaced. 'I could go to the authorities, you know.'

His chuckle sounded menacing. 'And tell them what? That you have denigrated your future King and now do not want to pay a man you do not know for your disloyalty to remain unpublished? Even if they listen, your sketch will become public.' His voice softened. 'Pay me and it need never come to light.'

Embarrassment scoured her very soul at the recollection of what she had drawn.

'Twenty-five pounds and you will be free of me for ever,' he promised, his tone wheedling.

'But I have just given you—'

'A show of good faith, my dear. Next time you will bring me what I requested or bear the consequences.'

She shivered at the sneer in his voice and a strange sense of familiarity. Had she met this man before? Or was she simply recalling his voice from that first meeting?

'How can I trust that you won't ask for more then, too?' She knew she sounded desperate.

'I give you my word.'

As if she could trust the word of one such as he, even if he did sound like a gentleman. 'No true gentleman would do something like this.'

His hand shot out and gripped her wrist. 'Do not insult me or it will be the worse for you. One last payment of twenty-five pounds and the sketch is yours. Think of your family.'

She swallowed. 'It will take more time to raise that amount. This was supposed to be part of it.'

'You still have two weeks,' he said.

It was a great deal of money to find in two weeks, even with the money from Lord Compton and the sale of what little jewellery she had left.

'I can't do it that soon,' she said.

'Two weeks or see it in every print shop in London.'

He sounded desperate. He needed the money as much as she needed this to be over and done.

She took a deep breath. 'It is not possible. Three weeks.' Surely she would have the payment from her publisher by then.

'All right. Three. Not a day more. I will contact you to arrange our next meeting. Do not fail me.' He turned and marched off.

Her knees felt weak. She put a hand to her heart. She felt as if she had won a major battle, even as she knew she had lost the war. She just wished she could be sure he had taken her seriously about it being her final payment. Because if he demanded more money next time, she would not pay another penny. And then she would have to face the world's condemnation. She blanched, her courage failing.

No! She must stand her ground, no matter the consequences. Except those consequences were not only hers to bear. No, next time he would return the sketch. She had to believe him.

Despite the trouble her knees had supporting her weight, she made it to the end of the alley and out into the lane. The walk to Westram Cottage seemed impossibly far.

'Lady Marguerite? Is that indeed you?'

She spun around, hand to heart. 'Lord Compton?'

He had clearly just emerged from the Green Man. What a surprise to see him in Westram since he lived closer to Ightham.

'What are you doing out here at this time of night?' His voice contained suspicion.

'I have been visiting a friend and am on my way home.'

'Alone?'

Now he sounded shocked. Men. They always judged one, whether they had the right or not.

'This is Westram,' she said coolly. 'Not the streets of London.'

'Allow me to escort you to your front door, my lady.' He bowed and held out his arm.

She would be an idiot to trust any man. He had come out of the inn. Men in their cups were inclined to be difficult. Neville had been at his most malicious when bosky.

'I would not trouble you, my lord. It is only a few steps.'

'It is no trouble at all.'

He was clearly going to insist. He did not sound drunk. He wasn't swaying or slurring his words. Giving in to him might be better than refusing and arousing more curiosity.

Meekly, she took his arm, but she was ready to run if he showed any signs of aggression.

They walked together in silence. For such a big man, he stepped lightly and matched his stride to hers. The lane became dark as they moved away from the torchlight on the walls of the inn. She glanced around nervously.

'Is everything all right?' he asked.

She found herself listening carefully to his voice.

It was nothing like the blackmailer's light reedy tenor. Lord Compton's voice was a pleasant rumbling bass.

'Everything is fine, thank you,' she said. 'Why do you ask?'

'Your hand trembled when you laid it upon my sleeve.'

Her throat became dry. Was her fear so obvious?

'You startled me, looming out of the dark that way.'

'I must beg your pardon, then.' He walked a few more steps. 'At this risk of sounding like too anxious a parent, may I ask you how you found my daughters? Were they truly co-operative?'

Why would he ask yet again? Was he trying to find some fault with his girls? Some transgression that required punishment? They had been so very timid in his presence.

'They did very well at their lessons.'

'And they did not plague you at all?'

She frowned. 'Not at all.'

'Good. They must like you.'

'They need more than drawing lessons if they are to be properly educated. They scarcely know how to write their names.'

Another long silence. 'I must seek another governess, I suppose.' He sounded unwilling.

An idea popped into her head. A way to get the girls out from under his repressive rule. 'Why not send them to school? There are several excellent academies in and around London where they can make friends with other girls of their age.'

As a child she had always wanted to go away to school after hearing Red's stories of fun and companionship. It had fallen to her to care for Petra, Jonathan and Papa after Mama died and she had been needed at home. Her drawing and painting had been the one activity that allowed her a bit of freedom from responsibility.

'No.' He spoke with such vehemence she drew away from him.

'It was merely a suggestion.'

'I went away to school. I know the sort of high jinks that occur out of the eye of the schoolmasters.' He thrust his elbow towards her and she set her jaw and once more took his arm. She could not risk alienating him. Not when she needed his money.

'I am sure you know what is best for your children,' she said as calmly as she could manage. 'I did wonder, though...'

'Yes?'

'Well, perhaps they might like to go outdoors once in a while. To draw from nature. We could set easels up outside at the edge of the lawn and—'

'They are better off in the schoolroom. They can see all the nature they need from the windows.'

She bit her lip. The man was impossible. 'Children need fresh air. They need to run and climb and experience the world. I am not surprised they ran away if you do not give them a bit of freedom.'

He stiffened. 'I will thank you to leave the decisions regarding my children's welfare to me.'

She bit back a sharp retort. It really was none of her business how he decided to raise his children.

They reached her gate. The porch lantern she had left burning lit their path to the front door.

She put her key in the lock.

He shook his head. 'What is your family thinking, leaving you to manage alone?'

How was this his business? Did he think to control her life, too? 'My lord, I am a grown woman. I manage perfectly well.' Or she would, if it were not for the man threatening to ruin her life.

The light from the lantern softened his features, making him look younger, and handsome, rather than forbidding. Her insides gave a little flutter of feminine appreciation. She froze. This was not a reaction she either expected or wanted. The meeting with the blackmailer must be playing on her nerves.

'No woman alone is entirely safe, Lady Marguerite. As a magistrate, I have reason to know this. Walking out alone at night is in itself a recipe for disaster. And, you know, I have a vested interest in your safety. My daughters would not like to lose their teacher.'

With a start she recalled hearing that his wife had been murdered while out one evening alone. And he was not wrong. Only moments ago, in that dark alley she had been terrified for her life. 'Then I shall be more careful in future.'

He bowed. 'Goodnight, Lady Marguerite.'

'Lord Compton.'

She stepped inside, then closed and bolted the

door. She leaned her back against it, listening for his retreating footsteps. She had the strangest feeling that he had lingered, waiting to hear the bolt slide home.

Imagination. He had no real reason to care if she was safe or not, even if he was a man who liked to control the lives of those around him. Besides, she would never be safe until she dealt with her persecutor.

Once that occurred, she would also be free of His Lordship's unsettling presence. He was far too domineering, too strict in his notions with regard to his daughters, for her liking. She could not help but be sorry for the poor little motherless mites.

Perhaps that was what they needed. A mother.

A handsome and wealthy man like Lord Compton ought to have no trouble finding a wife. A little stab of something pierced her heart. What, was she jealous of this unknown female and future wife? Surely not?

As she knew to her cost, good looks and wealth did not guarantee happiness.

Chapter Four

When the following Friday rolled around, Jack found himself glancing at the clock repeatedly. The hands seemed to move so slowly, he had actually checked to see if it needed winding. It did not.

He glanced out of the window. The storm from the previous evening had passed through and, while the sky remained overcast, the rain had ceased and the clouds were slowly moving off to the west. The weather should not be an impediment to his daughters' drawing teacher.

When the clock rang out the hour of two o'clock and then fifteen minutes past the hour and then the half-hour and Lady Marguerite had still not arrived, he began to worry. A cold dark place opened up in his chest. A sense of impending doom.

He fought it off. The woman was late, that was all. Ladies were often late. They made a point of it. And it wasn't as if she was travelling alone.

The butler poked his head around the door. 'My lord?'

'What is it, Laughton?'

'Nanny James, my lord. She asked if you would visit the nursery. It seems there is a bit of a contre-temps.'

Nanny had promised to once more have Lizzie and Janey in their best bibs and tuckers to await the arrival of Lady Marguerite. They would be getting restless. And when they were restless, they got up to mischief. With a sigh, he headed upstairs.

His oldest child knelt on the window seat, looking out. Janey was crying with her face in Nanny's lap. Nanny gave him a look of appeal.

'Ladies,' he said.

Lizzie jumped down. Her hair was a mess, flopping around her face, her expression held defiance and there were tear stains on her face. He frowned. 'What happened to you, Lizzie?'

'Janey said it was my fault Lady Marguerite isn't coming today. I said it was her fault. She pulled my hair, so I slapped her.'

Janey looked up. 'I punched her back.' She buried her face.

'This will not do,' he said. 'Ladies do not brawl, they, they—'

Lizzie folded her arms across her chest. 'They turn the other cheek. That's what Nanny said. Well, that is not fair. And it's not my fault Lady Marguerite didn't come today, just because I said I didn't want to draw silly circles and squares…'

He frowned. 'Is that what you said?'

Lizzie shrugged. 'I wanted to draw a horse.'

'Circles and squares make a horsey,' Janey said, though her voice was muffled by Nanny's ample skirts. 'Lady Marguerite showed us.'

'Lizzie, if you were rude to Lady Marguerite, you will apologise,' Jack said in his fiercest Father voice.

Lizzie's shoulders drooped. 'I want to draw a real horse.'

Perhaps this drawing-teacher notion of his was not such a good idea after all. Indeed, it had thoroughly disrupted his household.

'She said she would come today,' Lizzie said. 'So, it cannot be my fault she is not here.'

Jack recalled the rather stiff words he had had with Lady Marguerite last evening. Was it possible that was what had made her decide not to come? If so, it was rather unfair on the children.

'Did you say something rude to her, Papa?' Lizzie asked.

Jack winced. The child was far too observant. 'I don't believe so.'

'You did,' Lizzie said. She poked her tongue out at Janey. 'See. It wasn't me. Now *you* need to apologise.'

Dash it all. Hoist by his own petard. '*If* I said something Lady Marguerite did not find appropriate, I will certainly apologise. However, I don't believe—'

'My lord,' Laughton said, 'a note from Lady Marguerite. Peter brought it, just now.'

Jack opened the note. 'She is not feeling well. She has a headache. She will come next week.'

Neither of them needed to apologise.

'People say they have a headache when they do not wish to speak to someone.'

Heaven help him. 'Where did you learn such a thing?'

Lizzie frowned. 'Mama used to say it all the time. When people came to call who she did not like.'

He recoiled. His wife had said that to him on a couple of occasions, also. He had always taken her at her word. Did this mean that also had been a lie?

With difficulty, he controlled his rising temper. 'Nonsense. If Lady Marguerite did not have a headache, she would be here,' he said with more confidence than he felt.

'What if she never comes again?' Janey said, looking up from her refuge, her lower lip trembling.

Dash it all, he had paid the woman in advance. She ought to be here. And if she was ill, she was now alone.

The note did not indicate the extent of her illness. Well, he would damned well see for himself. He marched off to the stables. Having instructed Peter to return to Westram when he had eaten and rested from his long walk, Jack set off to discover the truth for himself.

Since the pain in her head was gradually abating, Marguerite made her way to the kitchen. Why she had headaches when it stormed she did not know, but they hurt so badly sometimes she could barely see. It was at times like this that she really missed Petra. Her sister always knew when she had a headache coming and provided the tea and the cool cloths for her forehead.

Well, now she just had to manage alone.

She poured water into the basin from the jug Peter had filled before he went to present her apologies to Lord Compton. She dipped a handkerchief in the water and wrung it out. With the storm long gone and the curtains in the parlour closed against daylight, she should feel better in an hour or two.

Would Lord Compton accept her excuse? Or would he dismiss her out of hand and ask for his money back? Her head throbbed a warning. She forced herself not to think. Thinking only made things worse. She took her cold compress back to the living room, placed the compress over her eyes and gratefully dozed.

A loud rapping sound jerked her awake. She removed the compress. What was the time? She sat up slowly. Her head no longer hurt, thank heavens.

The rapping noise came again. It was not in her head or her dreams. Someone was at the door. Slowly she got to her feet. Yes, she did indeed feel better. She parted the curtains to see who was at her front door.

Lord Compton?

She put a hand to her hair. Her cap was askew with her hair a wild mess. Bother. Should she simply ignore him? She glanced out to the lane and saw no sign of a carriage or horse. He must have left his mode of transport at the inn. But any moment now someone was sure to see him knocking on her front door. If they had not done so already.

He knocked yet again. Clearly, he was not going to go away until she had spoken to him. What did he want? Perhaps he was the sort of employer who needed to assess for himself the extent of an employee's illness.

Clearly, having paid her in advance, the man didn't trust her to keep her side of the bargain. She wished she had never met the man. Never agreed to teach his children.

She closed her eyes and took a deep breath. People were not exactly knocking her door down, seeking drawing lessons. No, she needed this employment. She had no choice but to speak to him.

The cap she tossed aside. She threw a shawl over the worn frock she had put on this morning in order to give Peter a note for Lord Compton and shuffled to the front door. Hopefully, she could convince him that she would be there next Wednesday and make him go away.

She eased the door open a fraction. 'How may I be of assistance, Lord Compton?'

He stared at her open-mouthed.

She remembered her hair. The colour of it, dark auburn, and its tendency to curl, often caused that sort of shock to anyone who saw it unpinned. She forced herself not to make a futile attempt to tame it into some sort of order. It never worked. Instead, she lifted her eyebrows in enquiry.

'I…er… When I received your note, I thought I should see if I could be of assistance.'

Did he really expect her to believe that? 'No, thank you. I have everything I need.' She made to close the door.

He put out a hand, holding it open. 'May I send for a doctor?'

'I do not need a doctor.' She needed peace and quiet. And besides, even if she did need one, she could not afford to pay him. 'I shall be perfectly well by tomorrow.'

He frowned and stared at her hand.

She had forgotten about the sodden handkerchief she had used for a cold compress.

'Your note said you had a headache.'

He sounded accusatory.

She stiffened. 'I do.'

'Then it is willow bark you need. Let me make you some tea.'

She blinked, stunned by his offer. 'I can make my own tea.'

His expression became thunderous. 'If you could make it yourself, you would have done so by now. Please, allow me to perform this small service.'

Why could he not leave her alone? Dash it all, she did not want her neighbours seeing them having an argument on her front step.

She drew back. 'Do as you please.'

Oh, dear, was that rude?

Warmth emanated from his large body as he passed her in the hallway. For some reason she felt the strangest urge to lean against him. To absorb his warmth and bathe in the lovely scent of his cologne made from pine and something lighter and sweeter. She must be even more unwell than she thought.

'Lay down on the sofa. I will bring the tea to you.'

'Lord Compton, really—'

'Do not "really" me. I was married. I do know what a lady needs when she has the headache. I also know you are alone here. Allow me to assist you, if you please.'

Unable to find the strength to argue, she returned to the parlour and leaned back against the cushions. The sooner she drank his tea, the sooner he would be gone. She closed her eyes. A gentle hand on her shoulder startled her to full wakefulness.

'Lady Marguerite, your tea.'

She straightened and took the cup and saucer. The first sip was heaven. He had laced it with honey to take away the bitter taste of the willow. 'Thank you.'

'You are welcome.' He reached behind her and rearranged the cushions so they supported her head and to her surprise she found it much more comfortable.

'I occasionally suffer from a headache when the weather is stormy.' She owed him that much of an explanation. She had also noticed that they came more often when she was worried.

'Ah,' he said. 'Some sort of megrim.'

'Indeed. It is not so severe that I need help, I assure you, though I do thank you for the tea.'

He grimaced. 'My daughter Elizabeth was concerned that her behaviour might not have been exemplary and that you might have decided not to return. I assume that is not the case.'

'It is not. I will come on Wednesday as promised. I will of course apply the payment for today to Wednesday's lesson.'

'Never mind that. You can tack an extra lesson on at the end of the six weeks we agreed upon.

Relief almost overwhelmed her. She had been worried that she might not be able to pay her blackmailer being short of the money for one lesson this week. She realised he was watching her closely. Did he realise how desperately she needed that money? She hoped not.

'Peter will return later today,' he said and moved to the window to look out.

'There is no need, I assure you. I am able to manage perfectly well.'

'If Peter had not been here to bring your note, I would not have known you were ill and might have thought you had taken my money and absconded.'

While the words were harsh, there was a teasing note to his voice.

'Would you indeed have thought such a monstrous thing?'

He turned, smiling slightly. 'Likely not. I have the sense that you are an honourable woman.'

Surprised, she stared at him. 'I appreciate your confidence.'

'Good. And my daughters appreciate your lessons. Lizzie has promised to do as instructed.'

She inclined her head. 'Then I shall see you on Wednesday.'

To her relief, he bowed and left. What a strange man. Dictatorial one minute and smiling conspiratorially the next. She would have to make sure not to miss any future lessons with his children. She did not want him arriving on her doorstep thinking he could order her about, the way he did with the rest of his household. It was bad enough that he insisted she accept the services of his stable boy, no matter that it was to suit his convenience rather than hers.

The following Friday afternoon, a downpour of rain forced Jack to abandon his plan to inspect a barn on the far side of the estate and return home. He hoped Lady Marguerite had not ventured out in such inclement weather, though he was glad it was only rain and not a thunderstorm.

He had not seen her when she had come to teach the children on Wednesday. He had made a point of it. He had the feeling that his presence made the woman uncomfortable.

Hell, her presence made him uncomfortable. He could not stop thinking about that glorious mane of hair when she had opened the door to him, or how the gown she had been wearing clung to her slender figure. Once more, he pushed those images aside and got on with dismounting and leading his horse into the stable to be cared for by a groom.

Peter came forward to take his horse. He frowned.

Lady Marguerite must have come after all. 'Did you get a soaking, lad?'

The boy touched his forelock. 'It were barely spitting when we left Westram, my lord, and as Lady Marguerite said, a drop of water won't melt us. We b'ain't made of sugar.' The lad grinned, showing a gap in his front teeth.

A person might not melt, but they might end up with the ague and it didn't look as if the downpour would end any time soon.

He went indoors and changed into dry clothes. He found himself pleased to have an excuse to have a conversation with Lady Marguerite, which was nonsense, of course. He had been pleased when Nanny had reported that Lizzie had been co-operative with her teacher on the previous Wednesday and that Janey had followed Lady Marguerite around like a little shadow.

When he entered the schoolroom, the girls were not in evidence. Their teacher was cleaning off the blackboard.

'Good day, Lady Marguerite.'

She turned with a smile and inclined her head. 'Lord Compton. The girls are with Nanny having their afternoon snack.'

Ah, yes. He should have realised it was that time. He nodded. 'How is everything going?'

A crease formed in her forehead and her smile disappeared. 'Very well.'

'Good. Good.'

She hesitated.

'Was there something you needed?' he asked.

'I know we spoke of this previously, but at the risk of being repetitious, I would like to request that you permit the girls to spend some time outdoors each week.' She smiled. 'Provided it is not raining, of course.'

A cold chill entered his chest. 'We did speak about this before and my answer has not changed.'

She huffed out a sigh. 'I think you are doing them a great disservice. Yes, they are behaving themselves during their lessons, but they are listless. I am sure it is from being confined indoors every day with little to do and no exercise.'

Anger rose within him. How could she think he would endanger his girls by letting them roam around outside? And as for being listless, he had seen no sign of it. 'If they feel the need for exercise, they have the long gallery. That is its intended purpose.'

'That is what Nanny told me.' She shot him a black look. 'Have you set foot in that room recently?'

He had not. His wife used to perambulate there when she was *enceinte*. He had walked with her before the birth of each of the girls. Of course, they had been hoping for a son. He still needed a son. But he was in no rush. 'I have not been up there since my wife died.'

She winced. 'Perhaps you would be willing to accompany me for an inspection?'

No, he wasn't willing, but he could see she was not going to take no for an answer. Besides, if there was something wrong with it, he would have it fixed.

He followed her out of the room and up to the third floor where a gallery ran the length of one side of the house. A bank of tall windows ranged along one side to let in the light.

The air felt cool and smelled musty.

He stopped at the threshold and shrugged. 'It is as I remember it.'

'There is nothing here for the children to do,' she said. 'And look at all these valuable artefacts. They are a disaster in waiting.' There were tables and glass-topped cabinets full of ancestral treasures strategically placed along the inside wall and at intervals down the centre room.

'There is lots of room to walk.'

'Children don't need to be tiptoeing around among the breakables. They need to run and jump and climb. They need to learn about the world by exploring.'

The way he had as a boy. He had got into all sorts of scrapes, too. But that was different. He was a boy. Girls were delicate. They needed safeguarding not only from the outside world but from themselves. Look what had happened to his wife because he had not understood this.

'What sort of man are you that you cannot take care of your wife? A man has to be in control of his family.'

His father-in-law's question still stung.

No. He wasn't going to be caught out like that again. He was in control and his daughters were safe and sound inside his walls.

'Are you telling me *you* were permitted to run wild on your parents' estate as a child?' he challenged.

'Certainly not. My sister and I did not "run wild", as you put it. But we played outside under the watch of Nanny or a governess. We went for long walks as part of our lessons, both with our governess and with other members of the household. We learned about the countryside...'

'If you think this room contains too many items for them to make use of it, I will have them removed.'

'That is not what I am saying.' She crossed to one of the windows and reached up to unlatch it. Even on such a gloomy day, the light from the windows caused her hair to glint like burnished metal. Too dark for gold or copper, more like flames in the centre of the fire. He recalled the glorious mane of thick glossy tresses. He had wanted to run his fingers through it to see if it was as luxurious as it appeared. Now he wanted to pull it free of the tight knot at her nape.

She pushed up on the window. It didn't move. 'It might not be so bad if we could open the windows.'

His jaw dropped. 'It is a forty-foot drop to the ground. I had them nailed shut for that very reason. If they fell, they would break their necks. It is not safe.'

'It is not healthy for them to be kept locked up inside all the while.'

He glared at the windows. He'd ordered them nailed shut not long after his wife died. 'Very well, I'll have the blacksmith make bars for the windows. Then you can open them.'

She gaped at him. 'That is treating them like criminals. They aren't stupid. They are not going to try climbing out of the windows.'

He set his jaw. 'Can you guarantee they will not, Lady Marguerite?'

She shook her head. 'But—'

'Well, then, there is no more to be said.'

For a moment, he thought she would argue further. But he knew he was right and he would not let a pretty face convince him otherwise. A man needed to be in control. If he had been less easy-going, given in less, his wife would be alive.

Chapter Five

At any moment, Lord Compton was going to change his mind about letting the girls have drawing lessons. She could see it in his face.

Before he could do so, she marched past him and headed downstairs. It was time to begin the second hour of their lesson anyway.

He followed behind, his step heavy on the stairs. She tried to ignore his presence, but she could not.

She willed him to continue on downstairs, but he followed her into the nursery, where they found the girls sitting on the sofa with their hands folded in their laps as if butter wouldn't melt in their mouths. Marguerite repressed the urge to smile. She could only imagine what mischief they had been up to until they heard their approach.

Their father eyed them closely. 'Are you feeling well, Lizzie?'

The little girl looked puzzled. 'Yes, Papa.'

Lord Compton sent a narrow-eyed glare Marguerite's way. 'And you, Janey—are you well?'

'Oh, yes, Papa,' Janey said. She glanced anxiously at her sister, before beaming at her father.

'Good. Good. Now run along with Lady Marguerite while I visit your sister and Nanny.'

'Nanny and Netty are having a nap,' Lizzie said.

He looked puzzled.

'Netty always naps in the afternoons Lady Marguerite is here,' Lizzie explained.

'Oh. I see. Well, perhaps I will see her at bedtime. Run along to the schoolroom, Lady Marguerite will join you shortly.'

Marguerite froze. Was he going to dismiss her?

The girls jumped up and ran out of the room.

Compton looked worried. And even a little vulnerable. As if he had somehow let his guard down and he didn't quite know how it had happened. She schooled her face into pleasant interest instead of reaching out a comforting hand. He was a man, he did not need comfort from her or any woman.

He glanced at the window. 'About the long gallery.'

'Yes, my lord?'

'I will have it made more suitable for the children. I am sure, with the windows open….'

'It will certainly be better than nothing.'

He smiled tersely. 'Good. I am glad you agree. You will, of course, ensure they do not sit in a draught, and that the windows are closed when you leave. In case of rain.'

Good lord, he must think she had the brain of a

peahen if he thought she needed such instructions. 'I will, my lord.'

'Very well. I will prepare some rules for the proper use of the space, then we shall be sure there are no misunderstandings.'

The man was obsessed with rules. It must be something to do with being a magistrate.

'I will look at your rules, my lord, and if they are practicable and sensible, then I shall agree to them. Otherwise, we may need to have further discussion. Now if you will excuse me, the girls are waiting.' Heavens knew what they would do with no one there to oversee them. Besides, she could not wait to tell them the good news.

'Ah, yes. One more moment, if you please.'

'Yes?'

'You cannot drive home in this rain. I will send you in my carriage.'

The man really was trying to take over her life. Yet again. 'I shall be perfectly fine in the trap. Thank you.'

'Well, you may be, but Peter's mother would not thank me if the boy came down with the ague from getting soaked.'

'Then Peter may stay here.'

'No. He will go home in the carriage, if you insist on driving the trap. Which means my coachman will be required to suffer a dousing.'

He was making her out to be completely unrea-sonable about his servants' well-being. 'Peter would get wet if he drove me home and I would be without my trap if I take your carriage. I need to go to Oxted on the morrow for supplies. I thank you for your concern, but I prefer to drive myself home and I do not need your carriage following me. You will have the villagers wondering what on earth is going on.'

'I have another alternative to offer.'

'Which is?'

'Stay the night. Be my guest. In the morning, you can depart for Oxted with Peter and the trap, provided the weather is fine, that is.'

A chill ran down her spine. 'Stay overnight?' She folded her arms across her chest. 'No. Thank you.'

Why was she even thanking him for such a terrible proposition?

He frowned. 'I do not see—' A look of comprehension crossed his face. His back stiffened. His expression became dark. 'Lady Marguerite, I am not suggesting anything except that you have dinner in comfort and a bed for the night in weather so foul one would not send a dog outside. You may, you can avail yourself of the governess's suite of rooms next to the nursery. The doors have bolts on the inside.'

He looked so irritated, so shocked, she almost giggled. Until she was overtaken by sadness. Yes, she had entertained the thought, however briefly, that he might have an ulterior motive in asking her to stay, but she was far too long in the tooth for that to happen. And she should be glad of it, too. She was glad. Wasn't she?

Then why did she have this odd feeling of disappointment, a sense that a hope had been dashed?

Nonsense.

Yes, he was handsome, but he also ruled his household with an iron hand. An ill omen for any woman.

She went to the window and looked out. He was right, it was pouring and the wind had picked up. Driving home in an open trap would be unpleasant and also foolish. She turned to face him. 'Why don't we see how it is when it is time for me to go home?' With Neville, procrastination had often worked in her favour. Half the time he would forget all about his demand. The other half, she simply had to grin and bear whatever it was he had insisted upon.

Fortunately, Lord Compton did not have the authority to make her do as he bid.

Still, she did not want to seem too intransigent. There had been enough of those sorts of discussions already. Push him too far and he might well cancel the girls' lessons.

'Very well,' he said. 'If that is what you wish, I will agree. But, believe me, I will not permit you to go home in a downpour.'

Permit? Her temper flared. All her good intentions flew out of the window. 'I do not believe I answer to you with regard to what I do in my personal hours, Lord Compton.'

He glared at her. 'Why do women have to be so... irrational?'

He stomped off.

Coward. He might at least have allowed her to reply to that bit of nonsense.

She glanced out of the window again. All she could hope was for the weather to clear up in an hour or two. At least it wasn't a thunderstorm or she might find herself unable to fulfil her duties or drive herself home.

Why not let her drive home in the rain? Why the devil was he bothering? The woman was nothing to him. The only reason he was concerned at all was because if she became ill, or, heaven forbid, suffered some sort of accident, his girls would be sad.

What other reason could he have? He didn't like the woman. She was far too combative. If she wasn't so dashed pretty… And that hair of hers…

Devil take it, he did not want to think about the way she had looked when she met him at her door.

He marched into his study. He'd much rather be out riding his estate than stuck in here.

He stilled, staring down at his desk. Lady Marguerite had said that about his girls, hadn't she? He had never been confined to the house as a lad, but after losing his wife and so close to home, too, he hadn't been able to bear the idea that something might happen to them. On the other hand, how would they learn about the world if they never experienced it?

Restlessness filled him, memories of his wife flashing across his mind. An urge to ride off to distant parts and never return struck him hard. Some days, he found his regrets so all-consuming that he found himself miles from home and in the opposite direction from his original destination. He understood why. No matter how often he relived their last few conversations, changed them in his head, the past remained cast in stone. Amanda had lied to him and like some bumpkin he had believed everything she told him. He also knew he could never leave his guilt behind, no matter how far he rode.

He forced his mind back to the present. The estate provided plenty of work to keep him busy. For one thing he had not yet sent an advertisement to the newspaper for a governess. He picked up the most recent copy of *The Times*. Perhaps he'd find one looking for a position and save himself the trouble.

He glanced idly through the first few pages, running his eye down the headlines, most of which held little interest. Balls and routs and fashion and a lot of politicking. And news of deaths in Wellington's latest battle. No one he knew, thank God.

The page of advertisements contained nothing useful. A few house rentals, the odd gentleman's gentleman seeking a position and a carriage for sale. There was a notice about a new sort of corset for ladies and a tailor touting his wares. He flung the newspaper aside and began crafting a letter to the employment agency he'd used before. He listed the attributes he expected to find in a suitable candidate to teach his daughters. Sobriety. Intellect. A good speaking voice. Someone with connections to society. Ability to teach painting and drawing as well as reading and needlework. Able to conduct sensible conversations on suitable topics. Someone who would care about the welfare of his children's bodies as well as their minds...

He frowned. It seemed he'd described Lady Marguerite to a T, apart from her physical attributes, of course, like a slender figure, a luxurious mane of red hair and a face that was not only pretty, but also held kindness. Green eyes would also be perfect.

He sat back in his chair and shook his head. This was so unlike him. He couldn't remember the last time he'd taken notice of a woman's *attributes*. He'd been far too busy looking after his estate and his children. To be honest, he'd been far too wary of getting involved. The pain of losing Amanda and knowing he was partially at fault was something he never wanted to repeat.

When he married, as he eventually must, he would choose someone he could trust to do exactly as he asked. As long as they were kind to his girls and were content to give him his heir, there was nothing more he would need from a wife.

He signed the letter, franked it and addressed it. He put it on the tray his butler would collect later and have taken to the post office. He moved on to answer his correspondence. The pile on the tray grew as the hour wore on.

The next time he looked up it was because of the clock striking four. Rain beat against the window and from the look of the trees the wind had worsened.

He straightened his shoulders. This was one battle Lady Marguerite would not win.

* * *

The housekeeper entered the schoolroom a few minutes after the children had finished their lessons and returned to the nursery. Marguerite closed the cupboard door and smiled at the woman. 'Mrs York, how may I help you?'

The woman dipped a curtsy. 'The weather being so terrible, Lord Compton thought you might prefer to spend the night. He said he would be pleased to see you at dinner after the children are put to bed. I am to show you to your suite of rooms.'

Marguerite's heart gave an odd little jolt. Her breathing quickened. He could not make her stay against her will.

Yet it all sounded so very ordinary. So normal. It was exactly what she would have done in the same circumstances. And the fact that it was the housekeeper delivering the message proved there was nothing underhanded about the invitation. Didn't it?

'I've assigned Lucy, the parlourmaid, to serve you, my lady,' the housekeeper continued. 'I hope that meets with your approval.'

It wasn't quite ordinary. It wasn't usual for a paid employee to be addressed in such formal terms by the housekeeper. Under normal circumstances they would have been equals, though certainly governesses tended to be treated more like guests than other servants. But they were not treated like family, nor did they usually have titles.

She could either refuse and have Lord Compton up here making a fuss, which would be noted, remarked upon and gossiped about until it had travelled all over the county and likely beyond, or she could simply take the offer at face value. His Lordship knew this, of course. He had engineered her acceptance very nicely.

But he had asked, not demanded or insisted. That had to count for something.

'The weather is terrible, is it not? Unfortunately, I did not come prepared to spend the night and have no change of clothing.' Nor any night attire for that matter. Or her brushes. Well, what could not be cured must be endured. 'It might be better if I took dinner in my room, if it would not be too much trouble for the household.' She smiled sweetly at the woman.

'Oh, you do not need to worry about that, my lady. His Lordship's aunt left some of her wardrobe here last time she visited. You are close to her in size, I should think. I have had them moved into your chamber. The rooms are just at the other end of this corridor, if I may show you the way?'

Her heart gave an odd little thump. Her stomach churned. Was she really going to do this? It was only one night. And she really did not fancy getting soaked to the skin. So, yes, she was not going to be missish. She would stay.

Marguerite picked up the slates and put them on her desk. 'Lead the way, Mrs York.'

In the rooms she had been assigned, everything was ready for her arrival. The maid, a plump, pleasant-faced girl with mousy-brown hair and freckles on her snub nose, dipped a curtsy as Marguerite entered. The suite was beautifully appointed at the end of the nursery corridor. There was a sitting room and a bedchamber and a small dressing room with a chest of drawers. While modestly furnished, the items were of good quality and the bed looked soft and inviting.

The windows looked out over the park, though with the rain coming down in sheets, she could see little more than the formal garden directly below. Whoever had assigned this suite of rooms to a mere governess had been generous indeed.

The gown laid out on the bed seemed perfectly suitable for dinner in the country. Well made, of good cloth, it was modest and sensible. There was nothing about it she could object to, even if the neck was cut a little lower across the bosom than her own gowns and the flounces at the hem just a little more flamboyant than her normal style.

'If there is anything you need,' Mrs York said, 'tell Lucy or me and I shall be pleased to see to it.'

'Thank you,' Marguerite said. 'Please tell His Lordship I accept his invitation to join him for dinner.' She smiled at Lucy. 'Thank you for agreeing to assist me.'

The maid smiled cheerfully. 'Happy to do it, I am, my lady.'

Mrs York left them to it.

'Shall I dress your hair, my lady?' Lucy asked.

Marguerite seated herself before the mirror. A worried reflection stared back at her. It had been ages since she'd had dinner with a gentleman who was not family. Not since she and Petra had entertained Lord Longhurst, now her brother-in-law, when Petra had been plotting to get him to hire Mrs Stone as his cook.

That had been a different situation. She and her sister had served as each other's chaperon. On the other hand, Lord Compton seemed bent on observing the proprieties, so where was the harm? She was a widow, after all. And not subject to the same rules as a single lady. It would also be a very pleasant change to have some company with her meal. 'I think only a pin or two is required,' she said.

The young woman nodded and set to work. 'What beautiful hair you have, my lady. Such a colour it is.'

'I don't know about beautiful. It is difficult to manage.'

'Thick and curly. My next sister down says the same thing about hers. Mine is as straight as a yard of pump water.' She chuckled.

'Do you have many siblings, Lucy?'

'Seventeen of us, my lady, not counting the ones who died.'

Marguerite's jaw dropped. 'Seventeen.'

'Yes, my lady. All younger. Spent a lot of time helping me ma, I did. I was glad to get employment here, I was. Maisie took over at home.'

Seventeen! Marguerite could not imagine it. 'Is your mother still living?'

'Oh, yes, my lady.' Lucy beamed. 'Healthy as a horse, she is. And happy to get money from me every week.'

Having fastened her cap over her neatly pinned hair, Marguerite headed downstairs.

Passing the schoolroom, she paused. But, no. Nanny would likely not appreciate the interruption if the girls were at dinner. She could recall her own nanny, who liked everything just so and who considered the nursery her private fiefdom.

Once her siblings were too old for the nursery, she had quickly learned why it was necessary to keep strict order among a bunch of unruly children, for the task of mother had been left to her. It was one reason why she was glad she and Neville had not had any children. She'd already served her duty in that regard.

Which reminded her, first thing tomorrow she would write to Petra and explain that she had decided to give drawing lessons to supplement her income. Petra and her husband lived in Westram. Marguerite's visits to Lord Compton would come to her attention the moment she returned from Bath. It was impossible to hide much from the residents of such a small village and she certainly didn't want ill-informed gossip coming to her sister's ears. Thank goodness her sister would not be as judgemental as the rest of the world.

She would write to Carrie, too. Although no longer considered family, since she had married a Gilmore, the sisters remained as close as before. Marguerite knew she could rely on Carrie and her husband, Avery, as much as she could rely on Petra. Which was why she could not allow that horrible man to print that picture and destroy their lives as well as hers.

At the bottom of the stairs, a footman was waiting to escort her to the drawing room. Lord Compton had already arrived and stood by the hearth, a glass of brandy in his hand. He looked magnificent in his dark evening clothes, much less like a country squire and more a man about town. She felt like a country mouse in comparison. But then, that was what she was. An eccentric widowed country mouse and now a drawing teacher.

Lord Compton bowed. 'Good evening. Lady Marguerite. May I offer you a glass of sherry?' He gestured to a console where a footman stood waiting to do her bidding.

She inclined her head. 'Thank you, no.'

'Something else? Ratafia, perhaps?'

She didn't wish to appear unsociable. 'Yes, thank you.'

He gave a little grimace, but nodded to the footman, who poured her a glass, handed it to her and went to stand at the edge of the room, staring straight before him. He looked as if he was trying to fade into the wallpaper, yet Marguerite was glad to have him there. Again, she was grateful that Lord Compton was clearly intent on ensuring no one could accuse them of anything improper.

They sipped at their drinks.

'Are—?'

'Thank—'

They spoke at the same time and both laughed self-consciously.

'Please,' Compton said, with a slight bow. 'Continue.'

'Thank you for the offer of a bed for the night. I do not think this rain intends to let up before morning.'

'You are welcome, Lady Marguerite. I hope you found your rooms to your satisfaction.'

'Indeed, I did. They are delightful. I only wish I could see more of the view. It looks out in a different direction than the schoolroom.'

He nodded briefly. 'The park was laid out by Capability Brown. It does not matter from which window in the house you look out, the views are splendid.'

'Perhaps the rain will have cleared out by morning and I will be able to appreciate it fully.'

'Do you paint landscapes?'

She was surprised by the seriousness of the question. Many men, and women, too, assumed drawing and painting were hobbies, something for a lady to engage in to while away the time. Only the paintings done by men were taken seriously. 'I have tried all branches of the art,' she said, 'but I rarely do that sort of painting any more. I mostly draw and paint botanicals.'

He looked surprised. 'The kind one finds in books about plants.'

'Yes.'

'Are they considered art?' Puzzlement filled his voice.

'They are illustrations, primarily. For academic treatises. An engraver uses them to create the blocks for the printing press.' And once he was finished there was nothing left of her original drawing. The process of creation was also a process of destruction.

'That must require a great deal of detail and knowledge.'

'Detail, yes.' The replication of intricate accurate detail was her forte. It was why her other works of art were stilted, as one drawing master had told her. Her need for accuracy sucked the life out of the work. 'Knowledge, not so much. I simply draw what I see. I am given instruction on how to dissect each plant.'

'I don't know how many times I have been grateful for those kinds of books and the artists who illustrate them, especially when it comes to the weeds that infest my fields. And pests. Do you only illustrate plants or do you tackle other species, like insects or birds?'

A warm glow filled her chest at his praise. 'At the moment I am focusing on plants. I...' She winced. Should she admit to this? Would he think less of her?

Why on earth would it matter what he thought of her? 'I have a contract for a set of drawings of English wild flowers.'

'Really?' To her surprise, he sounded impressed.

'Yes.' She smiled. 'This is my second book. It is to be published as a comprehensive guide for those who wish to know about the wild flowers of Britain and who wish to start their own collection of dried flowers. It will help them identify the specimens they have found.'

'Fascinating.' He frowned. 'I suppose that was why you were out in the fields when you discovered my daughters.'

'I was hunting for *caltha palustris*, otherwise known as the marsh marigold. They grow in damp ground.'

'I know it. I used to pick them as a child and bring them home to Mama with my feet all wet. Bless her, she always had them put in a vase, no matter how limp they were by the time I got them home.'

He smiled at what was obviously a happy memory. The smile changed his face from stern to gloriously handsome.

For a moment Marguerite could neither breathe nor think. Not only did he look handsome, he looked years younger, the lines around his mouth seeming to soften, his eyes lighting up. Blue eyes, she noticed. Why had she not noticed their colour before?

She struggled to regain her composure.

'Dinner is served, my lord,' the butler announced from the doorway into the dining room.

Lord Compton held out his arm and led her into the room. Three footmen stood ready to serve them, while the butler supervised the whole.

The table, a huge long affair as one would expect in an earl's dining room, was set for two at one end, the settings placed opposite each other. Somehow, despite the size of the room and the length of the table, it felt intimate. No doubt this was how a husband and wife would dine in this house. She could not help wondering if His Lordship ate his meals alone in this room every evening.

He seated her and took his place. The footmen and the butler saw to the filling of their plates and this time Marguerite accepted the offer of a glass of white wine.

They toasted the King.

'You must let me know when the book is published. I would like to buy a copy.'

Surprised, she stared at him. 'You would?' She could not imagine him collecting flowers and drying them.

'Naturally. I shall want to brag that I know the artist.'

She laughed at his nonsense.

'I am not jesting,' he said. 'You will sign it for me.'

She stilled at the words. Signing a picture was what had got her into a mess. She certainly did not want her name in a book where it could be pointed to and laughed at. 'I use a *nom de plume*. I would be happy to sign that name in your copy of the book.'

Hopefully, by the time the book was finished and in print, he would have forgotten all about it. But she could not help the little thrill his words gave her, deep in her soul. She did not need anyone to tell her she was good at what she did. A publisher would not have offered her a contract if she was not, but Jack's praise warmed her heart in an inexplicable way.

'How are your crops faring this spring?' she asked, knowing a man always liked to talk about himself and his own concerns. 'This rain must be cause for some worry.'

He put down his knife and fork, leaned back and picked up his wine glass, staring into the ruby liquid as if seeking an answer. 'I will be worried if this rain continues for days. We planted oats in several fields once the frost was out of the ground and rain can only help, unless the fields get so waterlogged the seeds begin to rot.'

'Let us hope that does not happen.' She had three more specimens to find and rain would make the task that much more difficult.

He put down his glass and looked at her. She had the feeling he wanted to ask her a question. She waited for him to speak, but he picked up his knife and fork and cut a piece of meat. Whereas she had been feeling perfectly comfortable, now this silence felt oppressive.

'Was there something you wanted to ask?' she said.

Chapter Six

Jack frowned at the forthright question. He really did not think he was so transparent. But, yes, he had wanted to ask why, since she was clearly receiving an income from her skill as an artist, did she need to offer drawing lessons to children.

Could the publisher be some sort of unscrupulous fellow who did not pay her as he ought? Or was there some other reason she needed money? Indeed, when he thought about it, she was clearly living hand to mouth in that little cottage. When he had gone to see her when she was ill, there had been no fire in the grate and tallow candles in the holders. What was her family thinking of, letting her sink to such depths?

Or perhaps it was the lady herself. He had noticed a certain stubbornness about her, which for some reason made her all the more interesting, but also meant she seemed unable to accept help. Had she also refused help from her family? Was she still mourning her husband? While she did not continue to wear widow's weeds, she did favour dark colours and severe styles.

And none of it was any of his business.

And yet… 'It must be difficult, waiting for payment for your work until the book is bought by customers, never knowing how much income you will earn.' Blast. He really should not be prying into her financial affairs. 'I beg your pardon. It really is none of my business.'

'Oh, no,' she said. 'I do not mind. It does not work that way. I am paid a flat fee by the book's author. It makes no difference to me how many copies are sold.'

Then the man must be paying her a pittance. He had the urge to seek him out and demand he do better.

'I see,' he said.

'The work is going a little slower than I had hoped. I have more specimens to gather and that takes time away from drawing. It is why I thought to offer drawing lessons. To tide me over.'

The clever puss knew exactly why he was asking his question. Clearly, she wanted to put his mind at rest. So why did he have the feeling she was hiding something? What could she be doing that she would expect would give him cause for concern?

As long as what she was doing did not involve his girls, he had no reason to feel concern. A suspicion entered his mind. 'Was it your plan to take my daughters with you on these hunting trips of yours?'

'It would not do them any harm to learn about

the countryside. I have never met a child of Lizzie's age who was unaware of the pain a stinging nettle could cause.'

So that was her reason for wanting them to go outside. Disappointment at this evidence of her deceit filled him. 'Well, she knows now.' Devil take it, he had snarled at her. He reined in his temper.

She smiled serenely. 'She also knows to look for a dock leaf to ease the pain of it, should it occur again.'

Grimly he glared at her. 'It will not happen again.'

'Because you will not let them out of the house, I suppose. It is ridiculous.'

Suddenly he was no longer hungry. The woman was making him out to be in the wrong when all she wanted to do was use the time he was paying for to work for someone else.

'I am not paying you to hunt for weeds, I am paying you to teach drawing.'

She stiffened. 'That is not my reason for suggesting they spend more time out of doors. I am thinking of their health. The development of their minds. Surely you do not want them to be fearful of—'

'My wife was murdered, Lady Marguerite. On this property. Not a hundred yards from this house, by a man who might have been satisfied with the theft of a rabbit, but to whom the clink of coin in a pocket was too much of a temptation.'

His stomach fell away. He could not believe he had just said that to her, out loud, in a tone of such ferocity she had frozen, her fork halfway to her parted lips.

He never spoke of this to anyone. Never indulged in self-pity or sought sympathy. His was the blame. The guilt. His burden to bear alone. He wanted to curse. To leave the table. To deny he had spoken at all. Instead, he took a long draught of his wine.

She took a breath. And another. 'I—'

He slashed a hand. Warding off her words. 'I do not wish to discuss it. Suffice it to say, I do not consider anywhere safe enough for my daughters, apart from inside this house. When they are older—'

'That is absolute nonsense,' she said, lifting her chin, her green eyes flashing a fire he had never seen there before.

'I beg your pardon,' he said coldly. As cold as the chill settling around his heart.

'Nonsense,' she repeated. 'There is danger everywhere. A fall down the stairs. A servant run amok.'

He glared at her.

Her eyebrows lowered in a scowl. 'With proper supervision they will come to no harm. While I am sorry for what happened to your wife, I hear it happened late at night. You do not suppose that I would suggest the children go out alone after dark. But just as they slipped out of the gate in broad daylight, they might easily slip out after dark if their curiosity, their need to explore, is not satisfied.'

'You know nothing of this. You do not even have children.' The woman had him on the ropes. He was fighting dirty.

She stared down her little nose at him. 'I brought

up my siblings, Lord Compton. I am no novice when it comes to the raising of spirited children.'

A punch to the solar plexus could not have winded him more than her confidence. He pressed his lips together. He was not going to argue about this with her. It was not her business. These were his children. His family. His responsibility.

'You brought up your siblings alone? How old were you when your parents died?'

She flushed. 'My mother died, not long after my younger sister was born. I was ten. The oldest of four. Papa never married again.'

'So, you took on the role of mother.' Sadness filled him. 'I see it in Lizzie sometimes with her sisters, even though she is so young. But your father was still in control of his family, was he not?'

She stiffened. 'In control?'

'He made the decisions? Hired the staff to care for his children? Set down rules for their care?'

She looked uncomfortable. 'There were very few rules.' She straightened her spine. 'But we survived.'

'More by luck than judgement, no doubt.'

'I beg your pardon.'

Devil take it, he had not meant to say that aloud. 'A man needs to guide the women in his household. Set boundaries.'

'You think they cannot set boundaries for themselves?' The steel in the tone held a warning.

'It is well known that women do not reason with logic. They think with their hearts. With their emotions.'

'Even if it were true,' she said with a smile that was a little forced, 'is it so bad?'

Bad. Look at his wife. She had known his opinion about her wastrel brother. Known that giving him money would only result in him asking for more. But her soft heart had taken her out of the house to meet him late at night, behind her husband's back. And her decision had led to her death.

A man must control his own house, or what sort of man is he?

'Yes, when logic is required. You know, Lady Marguerite, what I cannot understand is why your family, your brother, the head of your household permits you to live alone as you do.'

She inhaled a deep breath, her eyes widening.

Hah. That had taken the wind out of her sails.

'Permit, my lord?' Her voice was frigid.

'You have no servant. There was no fire in the grate when I visited you and, despite your fine gowns, you look as if you haven't had a decent meal in weeks.'

She gasped. 'How I choose to live my life is not my brother's business. Nor is it any of yours.'

'No. It is not. But my guess is that your brother does not know of your true circumstances. I cannot believe a gentleman would wish to see a sister living in such dire straits.'

'And I suppose you intend to be the one who draws it to his attention.'

The bitterness in her voice stopped him cold. He glared at her. 'I do not interfere in the lives of others, madam, unless they are my responsibility. I am simply expressing an opinion.'

Damn it. He wished he had not started down this road. Did he not have enough people to worry about, with his own family?

'Very well, I shall not interfere, as you call it, in matters relating to the welfare of your children,' she said coldly.

Finally they agreed on something.

Only it did not feel good. The fact that she had cared enough for his girls to offer an opinion had… pleased him in some odd way. The friendly atmosphere of a few moments ago dissipated leaving only frigid politeness.

She put down her knife and fork and wiped her mouth on her napkin. Such a pretty mouth. But it was set in a straight line at the moment.

'If you will excuse me,' she said. 'I find I no longer have an appetite. If you do not object, I shall retire.'

How could he object? He wanted to. He had the odd feeling he was in the wrong, when he knew he was right. How typical of a woman to turn the tables on him. It proved his point. Woman were illogical creatures. They needed a man's guidance.

A footman, blast his hide, dashed forward to help her with her chair, before he could come up with anything to settle her ruffled feathers.

Jack rose to his feet. He watched her leave with a surprising amount of regret. He had looked forward to this evening, but it seemed this woman was one with whom he would never find common ground.

He wished he had never hired her.

Heat burned in Marguerite's chest as she stormed up the stairs to her chamber. She could not remember when she had last been so incensed. The man was a complete— Bah. She could not think of a word. Yet beneath her frustration at his intransigence, she felt terrible sadness. The man was still grieving for his wife. He had cared for her. Still cared for her.

He was living in the past. And his children were suffering.

There was nothing Marguerite could do. She had reasoned with him, argued with him and lost her temper with him. That was as far as she was prepared to go.

Or it would be, if she didn't feel so bad for the children.

She passed the nursery door.

All was quiet.

They were such good girls. Yes, Lizzie had been a little difficult to begin with, but she was coming around. Marguerite was already fond of both of them. They made her laugh with their antics. And they deserved more than to be shut up in this house.

If she did not need Lord Compton's money so badly, she'd be handing in her notice first thing in the morning. Following his rules made her feel like an accomplice in his misguided actions.

She entered her chamber and turned the key in

the lock. After her argument with His Lordship, she did not think she had any reason to fear he would come to visit her in the night, but old habits died hard. Not that she'd been able to lock Neville out of her bedroom, but she had kept it locked against his horrible friends, more than one of whom had leered at her and made improper suggestions. All because of those drawings.

A fire burned merrily in the grate and she crossed the room and held her hands out to its warmth. She had not had a fire in her chamber all winter and this felt like an extravagant luxury, but, oh, so lovely.

A luxury that could be hers, if she married again. Marry whom? Oh, no, that she would never do. Nor would she consent to live under Red's roof as a poor relation. She and Red's intended did not see eye to eye on anything, as far as Marguerite could tell. In her opinion, Red was making a terrible mistake. She toyed with the idea of writing to him and telling him he ought to reconsider his choice of a bride, but that would be interfering. If she did not want Red interfering in her life, she certainly could not interfere in his. And while either of her sisters would willingly take her in, she would not admit defeat and throw herself on their generosity.

No, once she had dealt with her blackmailer, she would manage perfectly well on the income from her drawings.

Marguerite let go of a breath and removed her cap. She pulled the pins from her hair and set them on the dressing table. Lucy had set out a brush and comb for her. She had told the maid that she would not need help readying for bed and was glad the young woman had taken her at her word. Marguerite wasn't in the mood for polite chatter.

Marguerite had become used to doing for herself. She had decided she preferred solitude to inane gossip. And not having a maid at home, she had invested in front-closing stays. Fortunately, the borrowed gown was of the sort that had ties at the neckline and waist, meaning she did not have laces down her back. She undressed and slipped on the nightgown that belonged to Lord Compton's aunt. It fitted a little more snugly than she normally preferred and had a few too many lace frills and ribbons. She smiled as she recalled the negligees she and her sisters had designed. They had been so very popular with the ladies. Mrs Thrumby, who had taken over the millinery shop, had been shocked by the overt sensuality of the garments and immediately ceased selling them. It was likely why the shop had not been as successful as when she, Carrie and Petra had owned it.

She sat down at the dressing table and brushed her hair from root to tip. One hundred strokes of the brush. If she did not do this, it would be impossible to get it under control in the morning. Fortunately, she had washed it yesterday, so she did not have to worry about trying to do that here.

The slow strokes of the brush, the sheer pleasure of feeling her hair free from its pins and coming into some sort of order, dissolved what remained of her tension after her argument with Lord Compton.

This was one of the best parts of her day. As usual, the soothing rhythm of the brush made her sleepy.

A loud thump.

A wailing cry. From a baby.

She jerked upright.

The sounds were coming from the nursery.

She waited for Nanny to pick up the child and comfort it.

The crying continued. And continued. Another voice added to the racket. It sounded like Janey.

Unable to bear the noise or the upset any longer, she pulled on the dressing gown put out for her use and went out into the hallway. The noise was quieter out here. The baby's bedroom must back on to the one assigned to Marguerite. Why did Nanny not comfort the child? In bare feet, she padded along the hallway and turned the handle to the nursery.

The door did not open.

She banged on it.

'Nanny!' she shouted.

'Lady Marguerite?' a small scared voice responded on the other side.

'Lizzie. Open this door.'

'I cannot,' the child said. 'Nanny has the key.'

'Fetch her.'

'She is sleeping.' There were tears in the child's voice. 'I cannot wake her. I don't know where the key is.'

How could anyone sleep through the baby's screams? Marguerite rattled the door, but there was no possible way she could force it open.

'Netty banged her head,' Lizzie said. 'She has a big bump.'

Marguerite glanced around for some means of opening the door. Nothing. There really was only one option. If only she could find him. 'Try to comfort her. I'll be back in a moment or two.'

She ran down the hall to the top of the stairs, down one floor and along the other wing of the house. She recalled His Lordship had told her he slept on this side of the house. There were several chamber doors opening into the corridor. She banged on the first and got no reply. Dashed to the second and banged again. A door further along opened and Lord Compton strode out in his dressing gown, clearly not yet in bed. 'What the devil is going on?'

Marguerite almost sagged in relief. 'Netty has had a fall and she is crying. Lizzie says she is hurt. You must come at once.' She turned and ran back the way she had come.

Lord Compton caught her up. 'Where is Nanny?'

'Nanny is sleeping. The door is locked and Lizzie cannot wake her.'

He muttered a curse. At the top of the stairs, he caught her arm. 'Tell Lizzie I am on my way.'

She stared at him. 'Where are you going?'

'To get an axe.'

He tore down the stairs. Marguerite went back to the nursery door. Netty was no longer screaming, but she was sobbing between hiccups. Lizzie was murmuring comforting words. She must be holding the child on the other side of the door.

'Your papa is coming,' Marguerite said.

At that, Lizzie started crying. 'It's not Nanny's fault,' she said. 'Her rheumatics were paining her something bad.'

Oh. The woman had taken something for the pain. No wonder she hadn't heard the baby crying. She winced. His Lordship was not going to be pleased. 'Is Netty all right?'

'She was sick. Her face is white.'

Marguerite swallowed. That did not sound good. 'Try to keep her awake.'

Lord Compton came running down the hall, his dressing gown flapping around his legs, a grim look on his face. 'Stand clear.'

'Get away from the door, Lizzie,' Marguerite called out and stepped back.

One swing of the axe and the door swung open, revealing Lizzie's tear-stained face as she held Netty in her arms, and a scared-looking Janey with her arms around her older sister's waist.

'Well done, Lizzie,' Marguerite said. She took Netty from her arms. The poor little thing had a hugely swollen eyelid that had turned bright red and she was hiccupping sobs.

'Bloody hell,' said His Lordship. 'Where the devil is Nanny?'

'Fetch a cloth and iced water,' Marguerite said.

'Will she lose her eye?' Compton asked.

Lizzie squeaked.

'I don't know,' Marguerite said far more calmly than she felt. 'Fetch the water, then go for the doctor.'

He rushed off. A footman appeared a few moments later with the requested items.

Marguerite soaked the cloth and dabbed at the swelling.

A few seconds later Mrs York arrived in her dressing gown. 'Oh, the poor wee bairn,' she said, peering over Marguerite's shoulder.

'If you could take the girls down to the kitchen and give them some milk and biscuits, Mrs York, I think that would be helpful.' The children's eyes were huge and brimming with tears.

Mrs York nodded. 'Very well, my lady. Come along, my ladies. Cook made shortbread yesterday and I think there are a few left in the biscuit barrel.'

Janey took Mrs York's hand and gave a little skip. 'I love shortbread.'

Lizzie looked less sure, though Marguerite could see the longing in her eyes for the offered treat.

'There is nothing more you can do, Lizzie,' Marguerite said. 'I will look after Netty, I promise. And I will let you know what the doctor says as soon as he has been.' She glanced over their heads at the housekeeper, a signal that she wanted to speak to the woman as soon as the girls were settled. The woman nodded her understanding.

Jack urged his horse to greater speed even as he was mindful of the mud splashing up from its hooves and splattering the carriage. How the devil could his child be hurt when she was in her own little bed?

Jack cursed. He still hadn't received a proper explanation, but like a lamb had gone off to fetch the doctor. He'd gone himself, because the man would likely not come out in the middle of the night unless he realised the severity of the situation.

The doctor had certainly come willingly enough when he saw who was banging on his door in the pouring rain and had received a quick explanation. And now they were heading for Bedwell Hall at a rapid clip.

The doctor clung on to the side of the phaeton with one hand and pulled the hood of his oilskin cloak close with the other. 'It won't help your daughter if we end up in the ditch,' he mumbled.

'We won't.' Jack was so worried he didn't take umbrage at the doctor's implied slight on his driving. He was soaked to the skin, but he felt nothing but the urgency to get the doctor to see his daughter as quickly as possible. He turned into the gate.

It wasn't the bruise that had terrified him, though it had looked awful and he feared she might lose her eye—it was the paleness of her skin and its slightly greenish tinge. He felt sick to his stomach just thinking about it. How could this happen?

He pulled up at the front door and the doctor leapt out. A groom ran forward to take the horses and Jack followed the doctor inside. A footman was already leading the doctor upstairs, not even waiting to take the man's dripping coat. Thank God, his servants had some sense. And Lady Marguerite. Her presence of mind, her generosity of spirit in caring for his children…

But why was she the one to take care of them? Where on earth was Nanny?

He caught up to the doctor at the nursery door. His gaze sought out his child. She was still in Lady Marguerite's arms and had ceased sobbing. One brown eye was peeping up at the woman who held her, the other side of her face was ugly and swollen. Marguerite looked up at the doctor. 'I am worried she might be concussed,' she said. 'She fell out of bed and hit her head on something. She vomited before I got here. I have been keeping her awake.'

Dr Walker took the child from her arms and laid her on the sofa and proceeded with an examination.

'Where are Lizzie and Janey?' Jack demanded.

'I had Mrs York take them to the kitchen for hot milk and biscuits. A maid is looking after them.' There was an odd look on her face.

'I don't understand how you came to be involved,' he said.

'I heard the child crying. My chamber is the other side of the wall.'

'Thank you for coming to see what was wrong.' Where the devil was Nanny James?

'Do not thank me. Thank your oldest daughter. She helped enormously. Without her, I would not have known what was going on.'

He nodded, unable to stop watching the doctor listen to Netty's heartbeat. His stomach clenched. He could scarcely breathe or think. God, please let her be all right. He could not lose another member of his family.

'Go and get out of those wet clothes before you come down with an ague,' Lady Marguerite said.

He pushed the suggestion aside. 'Not until I know all is well with Netty.'

She shook her head at him. 'You and I really need to talk.'

Unwillingly, he withdrew his gaze from his child to meet hers. 'About?'

'About Nanny and her methods. It may be time Nanny retired.'

'The girls love her. To lose her would break their hearts—' He had suggested it once before, when he had discovered some mischief they had got into. The girls had wept and begged him to let her stay. What was a poor benighted papa supposed to do?

The doctor rose to his feet.

'Can we talk about this tomorrow?' Jack asked, his heart in his throat at what the man might say, given his serious expression.

Lady Marguerite pressed her lips together and nodded sharply. 'First thing in the morning.'

The doctor gave her a sharp look. 'Someone must remain with the child all night. I do not want the child slipping into an unconscious state and therefore she must be woken at intervals for the next twenty-four hours.'

Mrs York emerged from Nanny's bedchamber. 'She is still fast asleep,' she said, making a helpless gesture with her arms.

'Is she ill?' Jack asked. Was that the reason she had not appeared to assist with Netty?

Mrs York winced and her gaze shifted away. 'Yes. She is not well at all.'

'I'll take a look at her,' the doctor said. 'If Your Lordship would like?'

'Yes, yes, please do, but is Netty going to recover?'

'She'll be fine as long as you follow my instructions. As far as I can tell, the eye itself is undamaged. The cold compress has already brought some of the swelling down, but we must be careful with regard to the bump to her head.'

They would be careful all right. He would see to it.

The doctor headed for Nanny's chamber, followed by Mrs York. A few moments later he emerged, shaking his head. 'I am surprised she is able to perform her duties with her hands so gnarled and twisted.'

Jack sank on to a chair. 'How can this be? She said nothing to me.'

'She kept her hands hidden in her mittens,' Lady Marguerite said. 'She loves those children. I suspect she didn't want to hand them over to someone else. I wouldn't be surprised if she has other joints that are similarly affected.' Her expression softened. 'As we agreed, we will talk more in the morning. I have a long night ahead of me if I am to keep this little mite awake.'

How could she talk so calmly when his daughter's life hung in the balance? Besides, he wasn't going to trust anyone else to care for his daughters. Not after tonight.

'I will stay with her.'

Lady Marguerite's jaw dropped. 'You?'

'She is my child.'

'If I might have a word, my lord?' the doctor said, picking up his hat and coat. His expression indicated he wished to speak in private.

Jack escorted him out of the nursery and downstairs. The butler called for the carriage. 'What did you want to say to me, Walker?' Jack asked while they waited.

'Your governess seems to have a head on her shoulders. She seems to know what she is doing. Follow her advice and all will be well.'

The man had obviously not recognised Lady Marguerite and Jack was not going to correct his misapprehension.

The doctor pulled out a notebook, scribbled on a leaf and tore it out. He handed the scrap of paper to Jack. 'Have one of your men fetch this from the apothecary in the morning. Call me if anything changes in the child's condition, otherwise I will call in tomorrow afternoon.'

'Changes?'

'If you find you cannot wake her, for example. Despite the way it looks, I do not think the blow to her head was all that severe, but I prefer to err on the side of caution.'

'As do I, Doctor,' Jack said. 'As do I.'

The carriage arrived at the front door and the doctor climbed aboard.

Jack headed for the stairs.

Mrs York came out from the back of the house. 'Lady Lizzie is asking for you, my lord.'

He huffed out a breath. He wanted to check on Netty, but then he recalled the scared expressions on his older daughters' faces. 'Yes, Mrs York. Lead the way.'

He had no doubt that Lady Marguerite could manage in his absence. He stilled. It was a long time since he had trusted anyone but himself.

Chapter Seven

Marguerite glanced at the clock. It was nearly time to wake Netty again. It seemed so cruel to wake the child when she looked so peaceful. She rose from her chair and gazed down at the child. Her colour was better now and even the swelling was starting to go from translucent pink to a darker shade of red.

'How is she?'

Lord Compton's whisper made her start. It was his turn to keep watch, but the last time she had looked in on him he had been sound asleep on the daybed in the sitting room. He'd looked beautiful stretched out on the old *chaise longue*. He looked tall and imposing when standing and ordering everyone about, but lying down, with his bare feet hanging over the end, he looked younger and somehow boyish. She'd almost reached out to smooth away the frown on his brow.

'Did you sleep at all?' she asked.

He frowned slightly. 'I dozed, I think.'

Good thing she hadn't given in to her urge, then. How embarrassing that would have been. And she could see he hadn't slept from the hollows beneath his eyes. Likely he had not trusted her to watch over his child. And she could not blame him for being anxious. She had endured several sleepless nights when her younger siblings had been ill and Nanny had been perfectly capable.

'I will leave you to your watch.' She handed him the cloth she had been using. 'I will bring up some tea and fresh cool water before I retire. I have been bathing her eye each time I wake her. It seems to help with the pain.'

'You should not be put to so much trouble, Lady Marguerite. I will ring for a maid.' His voice was gruff, as if he was somehow affected by her offer.

'Why disturb them when I am already awake?' she said lightly. 'They all have their duties tomorrow and no chance for sleep.'

'Whereas you may nap as you please.'

Napping. It sounded lovely. She smiled. She also had duties, but they involved going home. But they would wait until she had caught up with her sleep. 'Exactly. Mrs York gave me the key to the tea caddy, when I asked her, so I can deliver on my promise.' The housekeeper had been a little surprised at the request, but had seen the sense of it. She also would not be able to sleep during the day.

'Very well. I accept your kind offer,' said His Lordship, his gaze drifting back to his daughter's battered face. 'A cup of tea would be most welcome.'

He frowned. 'I should have thought to bring you tea before I retired earlier.'

The man had a conscience, it seemed. Perhaps that was what made him so overprotective. She shook her head. 'Mrs York brought me a tray before she retired for the rest of the night. By the way, I have looked in on the girls once or twice and both are fast asleep.'

He glanced down at Netty and his expression was troubled. 'Thank you. It could have been a great deal worse, I suppose?'

'Yes, it could have been.' And those were things she intended to discuss with him in the morning. 'I will be back shortly.'

He pulled the chair closer to the bed. How easily he lifted the armchair and how much more convenient it was now. She wished she had thought to ask him to move it before he had lain down to sleep.

She quietly closed the door behind her and was surprised to find a footman waiting outside. He looked anxious. 'Is Lady Netty all right?'

'I think she will be better by morning,' she said, warmed by his concern for the child.

'Is there anything I can do for you, my lady? Mrs York asked me to stay here and be prepared to fetch the doctor should it be required.'

'I don't believe we will need the doctor again tonight, but you can assist me by bringing the tea tray up to His Lordship. Alfred, isn't it?'

'Yes, my lady.' The young man frowned. 'I am afraid the kitchen is closed, my lady.'

'Well, you and I will open it again.'

He grinned at her and together they went downstairs. While Alfred made the tea, Marguerite chipped ice off the block stored in the icebox and added it to water from the tap in the scullery. Another luxury. At her cottage, she had to fetch water from the pump outside the back door. The villagers had to go even further, to the public well in the centre of Westram.

She brought the bowl back into the kitchen and set it on a tray with a fresh cloth. Peter had the tea tray ready and together they took them back upstairs. Lord Compton opened the door at her soft knock. He raised a brow at the sight of Alfred.

'Mrs York asked him to stand guard,' Marguerite said. 'But I don't think it is necessary any longer.'

The footman looked at his master, who nodded. 'If I need you, I know where to find you.'

'I'll not undress, then, my lord. Just in case.' The lad marched off.

'Will you join me for tea before you return to your chamber?' Lord Compton asked, obviously noticing the two cups on the tray.

'Yes. Thank you. I will bath Netty's eye and then a cup of tea would be very welcome.'

He followed her into the baby's room. 'I need to see what you do, if I am to do it myself later.'

She showed him the way of it. He brought her tea and they sat together, watching the child fall back to sleep.

'I am not sure if I have properly expressed my gratitude,' he murmured.

'You have, my lord. More than once.' He seemed in need of comfort. She hoped her assurance helped.

He sipped at his tea and put the cup aside. 'Go. Sleep. We will talk more tomorrow.'

There was something about the way he spoke, as if he looked forward to seeing her in the morning. Once he heard what she had to say, he might be less pleased, but things needed to be said. And now was not the time. Once they knew Netty had fully recovered would be the time to tell him a few home truths.

Jack had gone to bed mid-morning, once more leaving Nanny, who had seemed to have recovered from what ailed her, in charge of the baby. The poor old dear had been mortified to learn what had happened. Jack had intended to dismiss her on the spot, but she had been so apologetic, so tearful, he had not had the heart to follow through. He had been horrified that her hands were affected by her rheumatism. She had become quite indignant when he pointed this out, and insisted she could manage.

He had, however, told her that Lady Marguerite would oversee the care of Lady Netty until after the doctor's next visit and that Nanny was to obey all her instructions. Fortunately, she had been pleased by the idea.

Jack joined Lady Marguerite and Nanny in the nursery when the butler came to tell him the doctor had arrived. He stood by, his mind churning with worry, as the doctor sat on the chair beside the day-bed and examined his daughter.

After peering into Netty's good eye and putting his ear to her chest to listen to her heart, the doctor gently eased up the purple swollen eyelid.

Netty squawked and squirmed. Nanny rushed to her side and the child quieted at her soothing words. The woman then had the temerity to give him a triumphant glance. He stiffened his resolve not to be persuaded by such displays of affection. His wife had pretended to care for him, then gone behind his back.

The doctor rose with a satisfied nod.

'I do not believe there is any harm done. The eye seems fine. A little bloodshot, but it responds normally to light. She was lucky.'

Lucky? He shook his head. He did not want to rely on luck when it came to the safety of his children. 'I still do not understand how it happened.'

Lady Marguerite held out her hand—in the palm rested a square block of wood. One of the children's building blocks. 'I think she might have struck this when she fell. I found it on the floor this morning.'

'It should have been put away,' he said, glowering at Nanny.

The doctor ignored him, looking at Marguerite. 'I think you are right, ma'am. It seems in this case all is well that ends well.' He picked up his bag. 'There is no more to be done except wait for the swelling to go down. As I said, if there are changes, anything you consider at all untoward, call me. Otherwise continue as you have been doing.'

Jack accompanied the doctor out to his waiting carriage. 'Thank you for coming.'

'It was my pleasure, my lord. I will send my bill tomorrow. At your governess's request, I have provided your nanny with a physic for her rheumatism. One that will ease her pain, but not send her into such a deep sleep the way laudanum does.'

Jack stared at him. 'She took laudanum?'

'You did not know? Between you and me, I think she has been taking laudanum for a long time. I am not sure she will be able to go without it.'

He froze inside. He should have known. Why had he not known? 'You think she is addicted?'

The doctor looked grim. 'I believe it to be so.'

'In other words, she is not fit to care for my child.'

'Well, I didn't like to say it. I know how attached we become to those who serve us well, but she is suffering a great deal of pain from her joints, so it is no wonder she needed something for the pain. I presume she was your nanny when you were a child?'

'Not mine. My wife's.' And the girls had clung to her after his wife's death.

The doctor nodded and they shook hands. 'Do not hesitate to call me if you think it necessary.'

'Thank you, Doctor. I will.'

Jack went back into the house. Laudanum. Good God, how could he not have seen it?

Lady Marguerite was waiting for him in the hallway. 'May we have that talk now?' she asked.

'Yes. Come into my study. We will be uninterrupted.' And there would be no servants to listen in on their conversation. It was the only place where a footman did not stand on duty.

The night before, when Lady Marguerite had come for him, her hair had been a beautiful mane about her lovely face. Later it had been plaited, the way a woman plaited her hair before bed. The sight of it had given his wayward body all kinds of ideas.

This afternoon, it was pinned back severely, in her usual manner. But for some reason he did not understand, it was no less erotic. Much as he liked to think he was in control, his desire for this woman was almost more than he could handle.

Which did not make a scrap of sense.

He went behind the desk and gestured to her to take the chair opposite. He stared at her for a long moment, trying to think how to phrase his question without sounding rude. Or too much like a magistrate investigating a crime. In the end he could think of no other way to ask than point-blank. 'Lady Marguerite, were you aware that Nanny took laudanum on a regular basis?'

A crease formed in her brow. 'Not before today.' She closed her eyes briefly, 'But now I think about it—'

Guilt filled him. 'I was not aware either. The doctor thinks she is addicted to the stuff. She is certainly not capable of caring for my children.'

'No, indeed. It was my reason for wanting to speak to you. Taking care of three children by herself is too much. And she has some very odd ideas about their upbringing. Apparently, she ordered that the children should have nothing but gruel for supper. Something about their digestion. Those children go to bed hungry every night. Which brings me to my second concern. She locks the nursery-room door at night and hides the key because Lizzie made a midnight foray to the kitchen. If there had been a fire—'

His blood ran cold. 'Why did none of the staff bring this to my attention?'

'About the food? The cook simply provided what she requested. About the other, the laudanum, I think Mrs York may have started to guess. She would have no doubt come to you eventually. Nanny is terribly sorry about what happened to Lady Netty. She was in tears over it.'

'She has to go.'

Lady Marguerite's gaze held sympathy, which after their argument the previous evening was a blessed relief. Their discord at dinner had left him unable to settle, which was why she had found him wide awake when she came knocking at his door with news of Netty.

'I agree that things cannot continue as they have, but to dismiss her out of hand would be cruel after so many years of service,' she said. 'And a sudden departure will only upset the children, who love her dearly, despite her odd ways.'

'I certainly do not intend that she should be turned off without a penny,' he said stiffly. 'She is of an age when she should retire. I will see to it that she is comfortable.'

She tilted her head, her lips curving in a small

smile as she nodded. 'I would expect nothing less, my lord.'

He relaxed, pleased by the compliment. 'I should have noticed something was wrong. I cannot believe I did not.' Guilt weighed on his shoulders. How could he have missed such an important problem beneath his roof?

'We all make mistakes,' she murmured.

Was she trying to comfort him? The idea that she might care to do so eased some of the burden, though why that should be was a mystery.

'May I offer a suggestion with regard to the children?' The hesitance in her voice gave him pause. It was unlike her to beat around the bush when she had something to say. No doubt it was something he was not going to like. Or she recalled the forceful way he'd told her at dinner last night to look to her own affairs instead of interfering in his.

'You may,' he said, rather more gruffly than he intended.

She took a deep breath as if preparing to beard the lion in his den.

'I think Lucy, the maid assigned to me, might be a good choice for the nursery. She has several younger siblings and before she came to work here she helped her mother a great deal. Lucy could help Nanny with the baby during the day and sleep in the nanny's room at night, while Nanny James is given new quarters where she can rest undisturbed.'

The woman knew more about the members of his household than he did. 'These are good suggestions.'

Her eyes widened. 'Thank you. In addition, the older girls need a governess. That should be arranged as soon as possible. Their education is falling behind.'

An idea struck him. It stole his breath. It was so outrageous he almost refrained from asking, yet he could not stop himself. 'Lady Marguerite, I know this is a horrible imposition, but would you consider becoming my children's governess?'

Her jaw dropped. Her eyes widened. 'Me?'

'I have duties that call me from one end of the estate to the other. I need someone I can trust.' And he did trust her. As much as he trusted any woman.

'I am sorry, my lord. I do not think—'

'I will pay you double the rate you charge for drawing lessons.' He held his breath when her jaw dropped, just a fraction.

More money would solve all Marguerite's problems. She would be able to pay off her blackmailer once and for all and perhaps there would be enough left over to buy good quality art supplies… But she would be taking advantage of Lord Compton's worry for his children. It would not be fair or right. 'I do not think—'

'You said you brought up your siblings.'

'Yes. In the way of a mother. Not a teacher. I am qualified to teach drawing. That is my area of expertise. But as for the rest of it—'

His brow furrowed. 'You had a governess, did you

not? You can pass along what you learned? It seems a simple matter to me.'

'Certainly not. It is years since I was in the schoolroom and your girls deserve far better.'

'It is a temporary arrangement I am seeking. Until a suitable applicant shows up.'

The temptation was too, too much. She tried to hold her ground. 'The work for my publisher requires a great deal of my time,' she said weakly.

'We can come to some sort of arrangement in regard to that. I need to be sure the girls are safe. I have to be honest with you, Lady Marguerite. I trust you as I can trust no one else.'

Marguerite stilled. There was something about those words that struck somewhere near her heart. The ache was both sweet and terrifying at the same time.

She did not want to feel that sort of pain. Or the warmth radiating out from it. Yet what sort of person would she be if she refused her aid? Not to mention it really would solve her financial problems.

'A temporary position, you say?'

'Yes.'

This was one man she could trust to keep his word. She hoped.

'I sent an advertisement to the newspaper for a governess yesterday,' he said as if he read her mind, or saw her doubts in her face.

'So, it will likely be three or four weeks before you have someone hired and in place.'

He nodded. 'To get the right sort of person. This

time I must be sure she is up to the task. The last two left after only a very short time.'

'Did they say why?'

He winced. 'The girls did not behave as they ought and the ladies were not pleased with my refusal to allow them to be given the strap. It is one of my rules.'

'Your rules? The same ones you gave to me?'

He looked…embarrassed? 'More extensive than those, I believe.'

He rummaged in his desk, found what he sought and handed over a sheet of paper.

She perused the list. It was almost identical to the one he had given her, except that it put Nanny in charge of the two older girls and the governess was merely in charge of education. 'May I?' she asked and picked up his pen from the desk. She struck out several items. The most egregious being the one about never leaving the house. She held his gaze as she handed it back. 'I will agree to be your temporary governess, if you can agree to change your rules.'

He grimaced as he glanced down at what she had done. 'This is blackmail.'

He had no idea what blackmail was. She shot to her feet. 'Well, I wish you luck in finding…'

'No. Wait. I—' He took the pen and added something.

She frowned at the change. 'You will allow them outside, but only if there are three footmen in attendance? One is quite sufficient.'

'Two.'

Heaven help him. But his wife had died in his grounds. No. Not died. Been murdered. She really could understand his fears. And he had let her delete three of his *rules*. 'Very well. Two.' She took the pen from his hand and made the change and wrote in the rate he had suggested.

He held out his hand. 'We have a bargain.'

'We do.' She shook his hand.

And just like that she had become a governess. 'I will need to go home to collect my things.' She rolled her lips inwards, thinking it through. 'I will tell Mr Barker to forward my mail on to my sister at Compton Manor. She will forward them to me here, once she returns from Bath.'

He frowned. 'So much subterfuge. Is it necessary?' He did not sound pleased.

'I have my reputation to consider, my lord.' And Red would be furious with her if he ever found out. Not that he really had a say in the matter, but she hated to upset him.

The biggest problem was her assignation with the blackmailer. She must not miss that.

'Then I must thank you, Lady Marguerite, for agreeing to help me. Knowing you will care for my girls, as I would myself, is a great weight off my mind. Also...'

What would he ask of her next? She found herself curious, to say the least.

'Once I have the applications for the position of governess, I wonder if you would be good enough to assist me in making the selection?'

She raised her eyebrows. 'You mean you trust the judgement of a woman in this regard?'

He frowned. 'Not just any woman, Lady Marguerite. But I do trust yours, I believe. At the very least, we can review them together. I will, of course, make the final decision.'

'And I, sir, will do my best to ensure you make the right one.'

He laughed.

It was the first time she had heard him laugh. It was a deep, dark, warm sound that seemed to start a fire low in her belly.

Excitement bubbled in her veins. Reason told her that taking this position was not one of her best ideas. Red would not like it. Her sisters would be concerned, but she felt…happy. Happier than she had in years.

It must be the luxurious surroundings which she would enjoy to the full for the next several weeks and the thought of finally being free of the consequences of her youthful folly.

She rose to her feet and dipped a little curtsy. 'If you will excuse me, my lord, I will go and impart the news to my charges.'

He rose and bowed. 'If you would be so good as to send Nanny James to see me.' He grimaced slightly. 'Perhaps you could assure her that nothing bad is to happen. That she is not to be summarily dismissed and so on.'

The man had a kind heart, despite his gruffness

and his rules. 'I will indeed. You may expect to see her in half an hour.'

'Thank you.'

Marguerite made her escape. Outside the study door, she halted and put her hands to her stomach, which was fluttering wildly. What had she done? Was he the reason—that smile, that endearing way he had of taking her by surprise with his kindness— that had caused her to agree to his proposal?

Certainly not. Yes, he was an attractive man. A woman would have to be blind not to see it, or dead. And she was neither. But she had taken the position for the children's sake. To ensure that his rules did not ruin their lives as Neville's rules had ruined hers. As well as to finally be free of the legacy of Neville's persecution—her blackmailer. That was all it was.

But the thought of spending time with the handsome Lord Compton had made the decision easier than it should have been. Smiling to herself, she took a deep breath and hurried upstairs.

Chapter Eight

Two days later, Marguerite had the girls' lessons organised and a daily routine established. With Mrs York's help, appropriate menus had been set up with Cook. Lucy had turned out to be a wonderful help to Nanny. The old lady liked the young woman and quickly allowed her to take over most of the work. Once she realised Lord Compton was going to pay her a generous pension which would allow her to live out her days in comfort, she had readily agreed to remain only as long as it took the children to become accustomed to her departure.

At the end of a long morning, during which Marguerite had worked on the formation of the letter *f* with the girls, she glanced out of the window. If only it would stop raining, she could put one of Lord Compton's rules to the test: his willingness to allow the girls to spend an afternoon out of doors. She also needed to find one last plant in order to finish the set of drawings she was working on. Provided they remained within the boundaries he had set, their walk might as well do double duty.

Unfortunately, the skies had been grey for days. If it didn't clear up soon she would have to seek her specimen in the rain. Why was she so hesitant? She and her siblings had never let a bit of rain stop them from tramping around the countryside, should they feel in the mood. Besides, they would not be going far. The rule demanded that they stay within sight of the house at all times.

Fortunately, primroses were easy to find. They grew in every hedgerow and ditch at this time of year. She was sure to find one or two at the edge of the woods that had been strategically planted to frame the lawns that surrounded the house.

She left the schoolroom and joined the children in the nursery, where they were waiting for lunch to be served. Their faces were bright and shining and their hands were scrubbed clean. Netty was also at the table seated on a pile of books, her purple eye startling against her pale skin. She was looking very proud of herself.

'I hope you don't mind, my lady,' Lucy said clearly, seeing Marguerite's look of surprise. 'She is old enough to sit at the table.'

At nearly three, she was definitely old enough. Marguerite had been thinking of her as a baby, because that was how Nanny had been treating her and no one had noticed she was ready to join her sisters in some of their activities.

She smiled at the little girl, who beamed back. 'Bread?' she said.

'Say please,' Lucy answered.

Yes, Lucy was going to be perfect in the nursery and had been thrilled to be asked. 'I am going to take Lizzie and Jane out for a walk, this afternoon,' she said. 'Please have them ready after luncheon. I will let the butler know that we will need two of his footmen.'

'It is raining, Lady Marguerite,' Lizzie said.

'I know,' Marguerite said. 'Won't that be fun?'

The two girls gazed at her open-mouthed.

Lucy passed around the soup. 'Eat up, my ladies. If you are going outside, you need to eat hearty. You watch how Lady Marguerite does it and you will know how to go on.'

The girl was an absolute treasure and Marguerite noticed that Lucy, too, was watching to see how it was done.

Marguerite tried not to smile as she picked up her spoon. She delicately scooped up a spoonful and sipped at it.

The two older girls followed suit. They had clearly done this before. Netty made a wobbly attempt and managed to spill a good deal of it on her bib.

'Well done, girls,' Marguerite said, as Lucy mopped Netty's face and chin. 'The more you practise the easier it will get.'

They were almost finished when the door opened and Lord Compton walked in. His hair was plastered to his head and his face was ruddy as if he had been out in the wind. 'Good afternoon, ladies.' He bowed.

'Good afternoon, Papa,' the girls chorused, while Marguerite and Lucy added their greetings.

'That soup looks good enough to eat,' he said.

The older girls giggled. Netty patted the last of the soup in her dish with her spoon and it splashed everywhere. 'Soup. Good,' she said.

More laughter. Compton took the cloth from Lucy, crouched down beside Netty and swiped at the mess. 'You are supposed to eat it, not throw it about, young lady,' he said, but he was grinning and he dropped a little kiss on the top of Netty's head when he was done cleaning up.

He looked happier than she had ever seen him. A glow spread outwards from her chest. This man truly loved these girls. It seemed there was hope for them yet.

Inwardly she winced. Now she needed to give him her decision about this afternoon. 'After lunch Lizzie, Janey and I are going for a walk. Would you care to join us?'

He frowned. 'It is raining.'

'Not hard enough to keep you indoors. The girls will be properly attired.'

The joy in his face disappeared. 'I do not think—'

She tilted her head in enquiry and as a reminder of their agreement that she was responsible for the girls' education.

'I have other plans for this afternoon,' he said

stiffly, rising to his feet. 'An appointment with my bailiff.'

'Then I would be grateful if you would arrange for the two footmen to accompany us. At two of the clock.'

He grimaced. 'Indeed.' He bowed and left.

Marguerite felt terrible. He clearly was not happy about her plan. For a moment, she toyed with the idea of cancelling the outing. But that would be giving in to his unspoken pressure, the way she had always given in to Neville. She'd let him bully her out of fear of what he might do in reprisal. She was not going to let Lord Compton bully her, too. She was not afraid of him and there was absolutely no good reason why the girls should not go outside for an hour this afternoon. Indeed, it would do them good.

Leaving Lucy in charge, she went back to her suite of rooms. It had been agreed that the time between one and two was hers and she liked to retire here with a fortifying cup of tea. At three, her responsibilities for the girls was over for the day and she was free to work on her drawings.

It was an excellent arrangement for all of them. Little minds could only cope with a certain volume of information and instruction before they became restless and unhappy. And she needed time away from their endless questions and need for assistance.

Had she had such an arrangement when her siblings were also her charges, she might not have become so opposed to children of her own.

Though with the way Neville was with her, she would never have changed her mind.

The task of finding primroses had not gone as smoothly as she had hoped it would, despite the fact that it had stopped raining a short while after they had gone outside. The footmen had obviously been given very explicit instructions by Lord Compton and they were determined that she and the girls would not go off the lawn at the back of the house. They certainly were not going to let them take one step into the woods.

Exasperated, Marguerite had decided after half an hour of being blocked from her intended destination to return indoors. Lizzie, who had been running ahead and thoroughly enjoying herself, suddenly stopped. Marguerite frowned.

'There is a ditch here,' Lizzie called out.

Oh, great heavens above. The little girl was standing at the edge of a ha-ha. A straight drop into a ditch in the middle of what looked like one long stretch of lawn. Marguerite hadn't known it was there. Like most country houses, the feature had been designed to be invisible from a casual glance so as not to interrupt the view.

'Come back from the edge,' she called to Lizzie as she hurried closer. Lizzie skipped back towards her.

Marguerite closed her eyes briefly. The little girl could have run right over the top. 'Hold my hands, girls, and we will take a closer look.' They quickly obliged.

The feel of little hands clinging to her gloved hands was like a memory from the past. She had walked like this with Petra and Jonathan, until Jonathan had preferred to spend his time with his older brother. She recalled how she had missed him once he'd deemed himself too old to spend time with his sisters. She'd been hurt by it.

She gazed down at the two girls. Oh, heavens, she was going to miss them, too, when it was time for her to leave. She really ought not to let herself get too fond of them. If she did, it would make parting with them so much harder. When they reached the edge of the ha-ha, she peered over the top, making sure she had a firm grip on their hands as they, too, looked over.

'Why is there a cliff in the middle of the grass?' Lizzie asked.

'It is called a ha-ha,' Marguerite said. 'It stops cattle and deer from coming too close to the house and eating the shrubs and plants in the garden.'

'Is that a primrose?' Janey asked, pointing.

'What sharp eyes you have,' Marguerite said. 'It is indeed.'

'And there is another,' Lizzie said.

'Good spotting,' Marguerite said. 'Now, how to get them?'

'Ask Alfred,' Lizzie said, pointing at one of the lingering footmen. The young man who had been so helpful the night Netty fell.

She called him over and explained what she wanted, then handed him her trowel. He trotted off to a spot where he could pass around the end of the ditch and come back to where they were standing.

'The yellow flower there,' Marguerite said. 'Please dig around it so you can get all the roots.'

Fortunately, the rain made it easy to dig up the plant and Alfred was soon back with his prize. He looked at the plant and then at Marguerite. 'It is a mite muddy, my lady. It were better I carried it, since I am already dirty.'

The other footman smirked, clearly glad he was not the one who had been asked to grub around in the soil. 'Very well,' she said. 'Thank you. I think we will return to the house now.'

Alfred looked relieved. 'Yes, my lady.'

'That was fun,' Janey said.

'Can we do it again tomorrow?' Lizzie asked.

'We will be going outside every day,' Marguerite said firmly. But she was going to have to talk to His Lordship about the rules he had given his footmen.

The man was impossible.

Jack watched Lady Marguerite and his daughters return from their walk from his bedroom window. Lizzie was running ahead a little way and then running back to her sister and Lady Marguerite. At any moment, Jack expected her to take a tumble. He would have to add the requirement that she walk, not run, to his list of rules. As well as confining them to the formal gardens.

He'd almost leapt from the window when he saw Lizzie running towards the ha-ha. His heart had been in his throat. He'd opened the window to call out to her, but she had stopped and, clearly realising the danger, Lady Marguerite had held their hands before approaching the deadly drop.

Damn it all, he'd said she could go for a walk and he hadn't given a thought to the danger in the middle of the lawn.

All right, so he had come up here to keep an eye on them on their first walk when he should have been out visiting one of his tenants who was concerned about the water rising in the river near his house.

He'd also been fascinated by the sight of his footman digging up some sort of plant in the ditch below the wall while the ladies looked on. He strode downstairs to meet them in the entrance hall.

'Papa,' Janey said upon spying him. She held up her arms and he lifted her up. Her coat felt a little damp.

'What have you ladies been about?' He certainly wasn't going to tell them he'd been watching their every move.

'We went for a walk,' Lizzie said. 'And we found a primrose in a ditch.'

He smiled at his eldest daughter. 'Excellent.'

'Janey saw it first,' she said. 'She has sharp eyes.' She looked really puzzled.

He laughed. 'It means she is good at seeing small things.'

'Oh, like when Nanny lost her needle on the floor and Janey found it.'

He tried not to grimace at the thought of needles with sharp points. 'Yes. Like that.'

'I gather your outing was productive,' he said, looking at Lady Marguerite.

'It was,' she said, but she sounded less than happy.

Well, that made two of them. 'Run along to the nursery, ladies,' he said, putting his daughter down. 'Lucy will have some dry clothes for you and a nice warm fire.'

Lizzie frowned. 'I'm not cold, Papa. I'm hot.'

A breath caught in his throat. Her face was a little flushed. He felt her forehead.

'She is hot from running,' Lady Marguerite said.

All very well for her to say. How did she know it would not turn into a fever? 'I would like a word with you in my study.'

He thought he had spoken pleasantly enough, but when she stiffened he could see how she might interpret his request as an order. 'If you have time,' he added.

She stripped off her gloves and removed her bonnet, handing it to the butler. 'Actually, your request is most timely. I have matters I wish to discuss with you.'

He led the way and, once she was seated in front of his desk, he rang for tea. A tendril of hair had escaped from her pins and become glued to her cheek. He wanted to set it free. He wanted to set her whole glorious mane free to riot about her shoulders. He wanted to spear his fingers through those riotous waves, had wanted to since the moment he had seen them in all their glory when he had visited her cottage.

He became aware of her quizzical expression. The awareness in her green gaze. She was breathing faster than usual, her chest rising and falling in shallow breaths. She was as interested in him as he was in her. Nonsense. *He* had not been interested in a woman since his wife died. Why, he had barely laid her to rest... He closed his eyes briefly. Two years. She had been gone two years. Perhaps he had grieved long enough.

Surely, he wasn't planning to have an affair with his daughters' governess? *Temporary* governess, remember. A widow. His blood heated. His body stirred to life. Devil take it, what was he thinking?

'I will have a fence built along the ha-ha,' he bit out.

She frowned. 'Were you watching us?'

'I happened to glance out of the window.'

'You were spying.' There was an odd note in her voice. Not merely annoyance but a note of...fear? 'If you do not trust me...'

'It is not a matter of trust. I merely wanted to see how the girls enjoyed their walk. However, now we are having this conversation, I do think it better if you would confine your perambulations to the formal gardens, where there are no steep drops and help is near to hand should it be required.'

'Tomorrow, I will be taking the girls into the woods so they can learn about different kinds of trees. I want them to draw the different patterns of bark.'

He blinked. She didn't seem to have heard a word he had said. 'No woods. It is one of the rules.'

'A rule we are going to change. Nor are the footmen to be given instructions to prevent us from wandering where we will. They are there to guard us, and I accept this, but they are not there to control our every step.'

He got up from behind the desk and came around to her side. He loomed over her, meaning to press home his point, to show her he would not back down.

Instead of buckling under his fierce stare, she rose to her feet and poked him in the chest. 'Stand back, sir. You need not think to intimidate me.'

He did step back. Intimidate? Was that his goal? No. He just wanted her to see sense, that was all. 'I will not have my daughters deliberately put in danger.'

'Do not be ridiculous. I would never put a child in danger. You are the one putting them in danger. Not only are you making them afraid of their own shadows, they are not learning first-hand about the world around them. Do you think they will not rebel at some point? If that occurs, you can be sure they will unknowingly end up taking all sorts of risks.'

He crossed his arms over his chest. Why had he ever asked her to stay as governess? He should have known she would be far too independent minded to follow his rules.

Was it for the sake of his girls, or had it been for his own sake? His need for— He cut the thought off. He didn't need anything. He simply wanted his household to run smoothly.

'I am sorry if you find my rules too onerous.'

She shook her head. 'I do not find them in the least bit onerous. I find them illogical and ridiculous and unkind.'

His jaw dropped. 'Unkind?'

'To say the least.'

'Nonsense. I want nothing but the best for my children.'

'But you are going about it all wrong. They need the freedom to explore—'

Her mouth was beautiful, even if the words she spoke annoyed him intensely. He could not keep his gaze from her lips, from the way she formed her words and the way her little pink tongue flashed out to add a bit of moisture to them at intervals.

She had stopped speaking and was looking up at him. Her green eyes were bright with passion. Such passion regarding so simple a thing as a supervised walk. Her lovely mouth—it had been the second thing he noticed about her, after her hair. The finely drawn bow of a mouth that begged for a kiss. It called to him like no other mouth ever had. He could not help but wonder what those lips would taste like, how they would feel against his own.

Her expression softened. Her skin, so pale and delicate, flushed a bright enchanting pink. A pulse jumped and flickered on her throat as if begging for the touch of his tongue. His body hardened.

Was he mad?

He made to turn away, but her hand on his forearm held him in place. There was a slight smile on those luscious lips and a softening in her eyes, that made him feel…longing.

The only point of contact between them was her hand resting on his sleeve, yet his blood heated as if licked by flame.

She reminded him of a timid bird poised ready for flight even as it gazed at the seed it wanted so badly. He didn't want her to fly away and so, as he would with a bird, he held his breath and slowly, ever so slowly, bent his head. When she did not move, or startle, he brushed his mouth against hers.

The kiss was sweet, it was tender and it was unlike any kiss he had ever experienced. He wanted more.

She drew back with a gasp. 'Oh.' She touched a finger to her mouth as if she could not believe what had happened.

He caught her shoulders gently, held her in his palms the way he would hold a fledgling fallen from its nest, firmly so it would not hurt itself, softly so it would not fear. 'Thank you. That was delightful.'

'It was.' Her skin turned vermilion. 'Oh. I should not have said that. I cannot think—'

He stopped her words with another kiss. Something a little firmer, but still gentle. More of a question than a demand. She might take flight at any moment and the last thing he wanted to do was scare her off.

After a moment's hesitation, she relaxed. Her

parted lips invited his tongue to wander a little. He tasted her slowly. She tasted of rain and brisk winds and freshness. She smelled heavenly. Like damp earth and lilies of the valley. He inhaled deeply, knowing he never wanted to lose the memory of that fragrance.

She moved closer and he enfolded her in his arms, not capturing her, not holding her fast, but simply offering her an embrace from which she could move at any time. Now she was so close he could feel the rapid beat of her heart and, when her arms came up around his neck, he deepened the kiss.

The next second, she was kissing him back with all the heat and passion of a woman on fire for a man.

Chapter Nine

Marguerite revelled in the feel of his lips against hers, the way his tongue stroked her mouth, the way his hands, so large and warm, gently held her close against his chest, yet did not leave her feeling trapped. Desire rushed hot through her veins and she brought her body flush to his, risking everything for the most exhilarating sensations she had ever experienced. Her head spun with the pleasure of it.

She desired him. Against her every instinct of self-preservation that she had built up during her marriage, she wanted to be held by this man. Gruff as he was. Tyrannical as he seemed. Was there something wrong with her?

She pulled back. He released her swiftly, his hands dropping to his sides, his gaze warm, his lips plush from their kiss. He evinced no anger at her withdrawal, as Neville would have done, showed no indication he would make a grab for her. Indeed, he was already moving away, easily accepting what he must think was her rejection.

Disappointment filled her. Perhaps he did not like the way she kissed. Or found her presumptuous. She had not meant to invite his kiss. She had intended to tell him that their arrangement would not work, but he had been looking at her in such a way, with such warmth and longing, and his mouth had been so very enticing, she had been unable to resist. How could she have done anything so foolish? She must never let it happen again. It would be inviting trouble.

She moved away from the desk and went to the window to look out. The sky was already much brighter than when she and the girls had gone for their walk. 'So tomorrow, we will be walking in the woods.' She might be a foolish woman who kissed a man on a whim, but she was not going to back down.

'And you will take both footmen with you,' he said.

She spun around. He was looking at her gravely, but the warmth was still in his gaze. And there was a slight smile on his lips.

She did not have the strength or the will to argue with him about this. 'Both footmen,' she agreed.

'And of course,' he said, 'you will join me for dinner, this evening.'

'Oh.' She frowned. She had expected to take a tray in her room, for a governess did not eat with the servants. But, yes, governesses quite often ate dinner with the family in the dining room. Usually, though, there was a lady of the house. But provided there were footmen present, and the butler, where could be the harm? 'Very well. But now, if you don't mind, I will go up to my rooms. I have work to do and we did agree that the hours after three are mine.'

'We did.'

She dared take a look at his face. There was nothing in his expression to make her feel uncomfortable. He was not leering at her or smirking. He looked as he always did. More or less. 'And what happened just now was a mistake. We will not let this happen again,' she said.

His mouth tightened and he nodded. 'As you wish.'

It was not exactly as she wished, but it was how it had to be. He was far too tempting. She rushed up to her room.

The next few days settled into a routine for Marguerite. If the weather was fine, she and the children did lessons in the morning and walked out for an hour in the afternoon. Instead of the footmen serving as guards, they became useful additions to the party, lifting the children to see into a bird's nest in the hedgerow or carrying their art supplies so they could practise sketching a landscape or a tree.

Marguerite didn't take them far from the house, but nor did they confine themselves to the lawn or the formal garden. Although teaching the children was tiring, it was also satisfying and it certainly made a change not to worry about every penny any more.

What had surprised her most was how much work she got done in the afternoons after her duties with the children were over. Today, she had completed the drawing of the primrose plant to her satisfaction and had only to add the colour and it was done.

In the evenings, she joined His Lordship in the dining room for dinner over which they made small talk about their activities for the day while waited upon by the usual phalanx of footmen. After dinner, he would retire to his study, no doubt to indulge in a glass of port or brandy, while she would return to her chamber and the tea tray delivered there each evening. There had been no repeat of her disgraceful behaviour and she had been pleased to note that there had been no change in His Lordship's respectful attitude.

Perhaps it was because he had not enjoyed kissing her as much as she had liked kissing him. Her stomach fell away. Her face felt hot. He must have thought her quite wanton, to have thought of kissing her at all. He had certainly had no difficulty keeping his distance since that day. She sighed. Soon he would find a replacement governess and she could go back to her peaceful uncomplicated life. At least, it would be uncomplicated if not for the man blackmailing her.

She put her drawing implements away in the desk located in the corner of what she had come to think of as her studio, a room off the schoolroom with a northern exposure. Her easel, set up near the window, took advantage of the cool natural light. She was going to miss this room. She did not have nearly such good light or space in her cottage. She also was going to miss her little charges, both their mischief and their smiles.

When she had left home to get married at the age of eighteen, she had viewed the prospect of having children of her own with trepidation. She'd been taking care of her siblings for years and the year of her come out had made her realise that most young ladies had a very different sort of growing up. She hadn't felt ready for marriage, but being a dutiful daughter, when her father presented Neville as her bridegroom, she had accepted his word as law.

It had not been a happy union. Indeed, Neville was a horrid man.

She pushed the intruding memories aside. She did not like to think about her life with Neville. Certainly, when she did not conceive a child during those miserable years, she hadn't been the slightest bit disappointed. So, it was strange how fond she had become of these three little girls. She sighed. Now she was being maudlin. Perhaps it was a case of missing her sisters. Both had invited her to visit shortly after their weddings. Once her work for her contract was finished and she had recovered her scandalous drawing, she would start with a visit to Carrie in the north.

She would write to both sisters and tell them her plan. She knew they worried about her living alone and this would set their minds at rest. And likely Red's, too. She put the drawings of the primrose between the leaves of some tissue paper, closed her portfolio and went back to her chamber to dress for dinner where the tweeny, Nell, who had been assigned to help her after Lucy had taken over the task of nursemaid, was waiting to help.

'Is this dress all right for you, my lady?' Nell asked.

It was her favourite blue one. The one she had bought when she and Petra had gone to London together. It was not at all appropriate for a governess having dinner with her employer.

Marguerite removed the apron she had worn over her gown while working. 'The grey one will be fine.' The neck came to her throat and had a small lace collar, its sleeves covered her arms to the wrist and its skirts were straight and unadorned.

Nell looked disappointed.

Marguerite smothered a smile. 'If you would be so good as to brush and pin up my hair, I would be most appreciative. The wind made a mess of it when I was out with the children this afternoon.' It had been deliciously windy. If it was the same on the morrow and not raining, she would see if there was a kite the children could fly. They would like that. Perhaps Lucy could bring Netty along, too.

She sat down at the dressing table and Nell soon had her set to rights. If the girl had added a couple of ringlets at her forehead and around her ears, what did it matter? There was no one to notice except a couple of footmen. And Jack.

She shook her head at herself. She had to stop thinking of him as Jack. If she did not, she was bound to blurt it out at some inopportune moment. 'Oh, my goodness, is that the time?' If she did not hurry she was going to be late. She gathered up her shawl, also grey, and went down to the drawing room.

Jack had his back to her when she entered. He turned with a devastatingly handsome smile. 'Here you are.'

The joy in his voice caused her heart to tumble over. Heat rushed to her face and she knew she was blushing wildly. As if somehow that charming smile was more than a simple greeting. She wanted to hide. Instead, she dipped a little curtsy. 'Good evening, my lord. I apologise for my tardiness. I hope I have not caused dinner to be held back.'

'Not at all. Indeed, if Laughton's presence at the door is anything to go by, your arrival is timely.'

The butler bowed. 'Dinner is served, my lord.'

Jack held out his arm, then led her to the drawing room. It was strange how comfortable she felt walking beside this man, her hand resting on his sleeve. Neville had always made her nervous. Jack made her feel as if no harm could ever come to her as long as he was near.

Not exactly true, but comforting, none the less.

He seated her in her usual place. A footman poured water for her and wine for him and proceeded to serve their meal.

'Did my daughters behave well today?' he asked as he always did.

'They did, indeed.' She recalled her earlier thought. 'If the weather is the same tomorrow, I am going to see if I can remember how to make a kite. I expect one of the footmen can help me.'

He looked surprised, then grinned. 'It was windy today, wasn't it? Do you think the girls can handle a kite?'

Did he think they were made of glass? 'I believe so, my lord. I know I did when I was their age.'

He frowned. 'You will need an open space to get it up. The lawn would be ideal.' He hesitated. 'Have to stay away from the ha-ha, though.'

The man could not help himself. 'I will certainly make sure we do so.'

'You will be careful,' he said.

'I assure you, I can manage the flying of a kite.'

'I am sure you can. I was thinking more of Lizzie and Janey.'

'I will make sure they do not come to any harm.'

He looked doubtful. Was he actually going to refuse to allow it? She adored the way he cared for his children so deeply. It drew her to him so much more than she could have thought possible—it made it difficult to maintain a proper distance. For some reason, she wanted to put her arms around him, kiss him silly and tell him he was a good father, with good intentions, but completely wrongheaded.

Put her arms around him? Kiss him? Oh, my word, wouldn't that be a mistake? What on earth was wrong with her, thinking such wicked thoughts.

She changed the topic. 'Do you think the war will end soon?'

He frowned. 'I believe Wellington has it well in hand. I certainly hope so.'

The first course of roast beef with spring greens and potatoes *à la dauphinoise* was removed and replaced by a game pie.

Marguerite always made a point of reading the newspapers while she ate her lunch so she could hold a sensible conversation with her dinner companion. 'There have been far too many deaths over the Corsican monster's ambitions.'

'Indeed.' He gave her a look of sympathy.

Dash it, she needed no sympathy over Neville, but that was not the sort of thing one said. 'It will be good to have the troops come home.'

Jack took a bite of pie and chewed thoughtfully. 'Actually, that is something about which I worry.'

'Worry?' she said, surprised.

'The country will be faced with the sudden return of a great many men in need of work. Men who have served their country well. They will need employment or I see trouble ahead.'

'I had not thought of that aspect. Perhaps soldiers will be needed elsewhere. Canada, for example. Or India. Or even the factories in the north.'

'Some, maybe. But not in the numbers we have sent to Europe. I wouldn't mind a few more men on the estate, if they are willing to work, but I can't pay anything like the mills do.'

Dessert was a meringue confection with cream, which Marguerite declined. She found it far too sweet for her taste.

'Perhaps you would prefer an orange,' Jack said, indicating the bowl in the centre of the table. 'My gardener says we have a fine crop this year.'

'Yes, please.'

He selected one, taking a knife to the peel, dividing it into quarters.

There was something very sensual about the way his strong blunt fingers tore the peel away from the fruit and then pulled apart the segments and placed them on a small plate. He passed it to her.

'Thank you, my lord.' She pushed the plate back towards him a fraction. 'May I offer you a piece after you worked so hard on my behalf?'

He chuckled. 'Not exactly hard, but, yes, thank you.' He took two of the segments and placed them on his plate.

She bit into the fruit and was rewarded with a flood of juice and a tart tang of orange. 'This is delicious.'

'I know,' he said, looking pleased. 'Such a treat. I only wish I could grow enough to sell.'

'You would make a fortune. Oranges are very expensive.'

'Sadly, the British climate is too cold for them to grow out in the fields, so we have to stick to our apples and our vegetables. And oats for our horses.'

Which reminded her. 'Speaking of horses, I think it is time for Lady Elizabeth to begin riding lessons.'

Across the table, Lord Compton's expression froze. 'What makes you say that?'

'Because she is interested. She has mentioned it more than once that you have promised her a pony.'

He grimaced. 'I thought to wait another year or two.'

'The earlier one learns to ride, the better it is.'

'At what age did you learn?'

The curiosity in his voice gave her pause. He quite often asked these sorts of questions, as if he really wanted to know more about her, when she preferred to keep him at a distance. Tried and failed miserably if the way she felt every time she saw him was any indication. 'My father took me up on his horse when I was three. I rode alone when I was five.'

He huffed out a breath. 'Much younger than Elizabeth is now.'

'Yes. And she is wild to try it. It would be better for her to have lessons than try unsupervised.'

'Are you telling me...?'

'If you will recall our first meeting? It was the boys in the stable who had told her where to go to find the frog she was after.'

His complexion paled. 'Then I had better see to it.'

Poor man. But he was coming along nicely, if slowly. Beginning to understand that his children needed to explore their world, as long as they were supervised. There were other matters he needed to address with regard to his daughters, but she would save those for another time. 'I will let you tell her the good news. She will be so pleased.'

'First I had better get the pony.'

Since she had finished her orange, she rose to her feet. 'Goodnight, my lord.'

'Goodnight, Lady Marguerite.'

There was an odd note of sadness in his voice as he spoke. She shook her head at her foolish thought. She must be imagining it.

Jack always enjoyed his dinners with Lady Marguerite. Before she came, he mostly ate from a tray in his study and often couldn't recall what he had ingested. There was nothing extraordinary about the meals or their conversation. Indeed, it seemed ordinary in the extreme. They were polite to each other. They spoke of nothing of great import apart from his children and the issues reported in the London and local newspapers. Oddly, Lady Marguerite rarely spoke of anything personal. He knew as much about her now as he had the day she first arrived here. And yet he felt as if he knew her very well indeed.

She was a lovely, kind-hearted woman, who, while she was always calm and collected, had the shadows of sadness in her eyes.

Something inside him ached to lift her spirits He longed to make her laugh out loud with happiness. A foolish thing indeed.

He waved off the decanter of port offered by Laughton. He did not want to sit alone at the table or in his study. 'I plan to retire.' There would be brandy in his chamber and a cosy fire.

He rose and went upstairs, where his valet readied him for bed and left him to it.

He couldn't help thinking about Lady Marguerite as he sipped his brandy in the armchair beside the fire. She had very decided ideas about how he should raise his daughters and wasn't afraid to voice them.

He liked her spirit, the fact that she would care enough about his girls to try to impose her will upon him. He recalled his own boyhood. He had been free to wander the estate either with friends or by himself when he wasn't at his lessons or being taught the duties of an earl by his father.

Part of learning those duties had been riding out with his papa and listening to him talk to his tenants. Or joining him on a hunt. Or assisting him with the ledgers. Each year his father had let him take on more and more of the responsibility for some aspect of the estate.

He'd learned by doing. And it had not been all work. They had hacked out together and, yes, he recalled several occasions where he and his papa had flown a kite.

A very fine kite, if he recalled correctly. He had not seen it for years. His mother must have put it in the attic. He would send someone to look for it in the morning.

He swirled the brandy in his glass. Better yet, he would look for it himself.

He rose and tightened the belt of his dressing gown. The stairs to the attic storage were in the other wing of the house, the old wing. The attic in this wing housed the servants and though the two wings were joined he certainly wasn't going to go prowling around where the servants slept. That domain belonged to the butler and the housekeeper.

But there was no reason he could not see if he was right about that kite. That would put a smile on Lady Marguerite's face.

His slippers made no sound on the carpet as he went up to the third floor and past the nursery door. He paused for a moment, listening. All was quiet. The next door along led to the governess's suite now occupied by Lady Marguerite. As he passed her door, he heard the sound of humming. Lady Marguerite was still up.

On a whim, he knocked on her door.

The humming stopped. 'Yes?' she said.

Feeling a bit like a naughty schoolboy, he leaned close to the door. 'It is me. Jack.'

The lock tumbled with a noisy click and the door inched open. She peered out.

He held his candle aloft.

'Lord Compton?' she said.

'I have recalled where we might find a kite. I thought you might go with me, to ensure it is suitable.'

'Can it not wait until morning?'

It could, he supposed, but now he had thought of the idea he wanted to follow it to its conclusion. And besides... 'I have a meeting with a tenant early in the morning. I doubt I will have time.'

'One moment. Let me put on a gown.' The door closed. When it opened again he was afforded a view of a plain woollen dressing gown tightly belted and a woman with her hair in a thick plait down her back. Much as he wanted to stare at the delightful view, he turned and marched to the end of the hallway.

The stairs rising to the attic from the third floor narrowed so much Jack's shoulders would barely fit between the walls. 'Allow me to go first,' he said, looking upwards, 'and light the way. If all is safe, I will come back for you.'

He did not give her a chance to object, but made his way up and pushed open the door. He hadn't been up here in years. The light of the candles showed what an excellent housewife his mother had been. The dust on the floor was thick, but the area beneath the eaves was impeccably tidy. There were tables stacked in one place, chairs in another. Old trunks took up a corner.

He turned to go back for Marguerite and found her right on his heels. Damned independent woman. But there was so much curiosity on her face, he could only smile and stand back to allow her to enter.

'Over here,' he said, lighting the way with his candle until they reached the far end where he could see his old rocking horse. He would bet his best hunter the rest of his nursery toys would be with it. Dash it. He had forgotten all about that horse. Netty might like it. He pulled it out. 'I will have it brought down to the nursery tomorrow.'

He poked around. Tin soldiers lined up in little boxes probably wouldn't interest his girls, but, inside one of the trunks, there were hoops and tops. 'Would they like these, do you think?' he asked.

'I am sure they would,' she said. 'New toys are always welcome.'

'Nanny wouldn't have known about these,' he said, looking about him. 'All the toys in the nursery are new or were my wife's. These were mine. Put away by my mother.'

She knelt, looking through a box. She pulled forth a small sword in a scabbard. 'I think we will leave this one up here.' She dipped in again and found a box containing wooden farm animals and little fences. 'These, though, are perfect.'

Memories flooded through him of playing with the animals, pretending to be a farmer. He had been an only child and these toys had been his friends. He would like his children to enjoy them, too.

And there in the corner was what he was looking for, a large diamond-shaped kite with red sails and yellow tail.

He picked it up, turning it around. It looked as good as new. He gave it a shake. Dust flew. He coughed. As did Marguerite, who sat back on her heels and watched him dust off the kite.

'It is a fine one,' she said, her voice full of admiration.

'It is,' Jack said. He loved seeing a smile on her face in the flickering candlelight. She looked beautiful when she smiled. He fought the urge to kiss her. 'We will take it down to the nursery ready for tomorrow. I will ask Mrs York to have the other toys and the rocking horse brought down in the morning.'

'She should bring down these, too.' She sorted out

several items and placed them next to the horse. She dusted off her hands and started to rise.

He reached out and took her hand.

She gazed up at him as he brought her to her feet. They stood close, gazing at each other. His heart beat a little faster and sounded loud in his ears. Her hand fluttered in his. He was still holding it. He did not want to release it. But he must.

'Thank you for indulging me,' he said softly. 'We both know I could have sent a servant up here to find these toys, but somehow I wanted to be the one...'

'You love your daughters,' she said softly with a smile.

She understood.

Slowly, carefully, he bent his head to kiss those sweetly smiling lips. At the first touch of velvet softness against his mouth desire rocketed through him. He rocked back on his heels, putting a fraction of distance between them. 'Marguerite,' he said.

'Jack,' she murmured and put her arms around his neck. 'I swore I would not let this happen again, but I find you perfectly irresistible.'

He brushed his mouth across hers as if he could taste the words that gave him so much pleasure all his blood had headed south and his brain was scarcely functioning. 'Irresistible.'

'Perfectly,' she breathed against his mouth.

He pulled her close and kissed her properly and thoroughly until his head was spinning and they were both breathless.

Kissing her was wonderful. Better than anything

he'd experienced for a very long time. How could he have forgotten how good a woman felt in his arms? Not just any woman. This one. This lovely, pliant, gorgeous woman who kissed him back so seriously, so intensely as if her life depended on it.

He eased her closer, longing to feel her body flush with his and ease the ache in his groin. The part of him he'd ignored for so long clamoured for her attention. He rocked his hips against hers, while he stroked circles on her back and deepened the kiss. He plundered the warm wet depths of her mouth with his tongue and she did the same to him, tasting him, stroking his tongue with hers. His body shook with desire.

Without thought, he found the ribbon fastening the end of her plait and pulled it undone. He teased the twisted ropes of hair apart. He pulled back to look at the result of his effort. Wild waves of fiery locks fell about her shoulders. 'You have the most beautiful hair I have ever seen.' He let it slide through his fingers, stroking it back from her face. A shadow passed across her face.

'What is it?' he whispered.

She smiled, softly, regretfully. 'Do you not find it too red? Too wanton.'

'Good lord, no. I find it magnificent.' He took her lips before the argument he saw forming on her face could turn itself into words. Whoever had told her that her hair was not her crowning glory was a fool.

She stiffened slightly, then surrendered to his kiss. He'd noticed that before. That slight withdrawal at his touch, before she accepted it. She reminded him of a newly broken colt, not quite trusting, but willing to try. And so he took the kiss slowly and only when she was kissing him back did he pull her close with one hand on her plump derrière and allow his other hand to shape the curve of her waist, to gently explore the ribcage above and finally brush the lovely swell of her breast with the heel of his hand.

She stilled.

He let his hand move on, cruising her spine before returning to her hip and following the same path. The third time he stroked her breast he left his hand there and lifted his head. His cock hardened like granite, aching with need. If he didn't stop now... He gazed into her face. 'Marguerite,' he breathed, his voice husky. 'We— I— You—'

She touched a finger to his lips. 'I love the way you kiss me.'

The words were like a stroke to his shaft. The desperation in her voice shocked him out of his sensual trance.

What was he doing? His hands shook with the effort of not laying her down on the floor and burying himself inside her. She was a lady. A noblewoman. Not a courtesan.

He tried to step back.

She clung to him. 'Don't.'

Did she not understand what was happening here? The danger? He reached up and took one of her small hands in his and opened her fingers, pressing her palm against his hard member. 'This is what your kisses do to me,' he murmured against her mouth.

Her eyelids lowered a fraction, her expression softened. 'Then we both know what we really want.'

Of course she understood. For some reason, he always thought her innocent. She was a widow. 'Are you sure?'

A secretive smile crossed her lips. 'Very sure, my dearest Jack.'

His ballocks tightened at the sound of his name on her lips. His blood ran hot and wild through his veins. A willing widow. What more could a man want after years of celibacy.

A bed, perhaps? He certainly wasn't going to take her on the floor. Yet if they went downstairs, they were bound to run into some servant or other. Damn. He should have planned this better.

But he hadn't planned this at all. He'd simply wanted to please her by finding the kite. Oh, and he hadn't secretly hoped that he might also sneak a kiss? He did not lie to himself any more than he lied to others. He had hoped, but he had not expected to have his wish granted. Not after last time.

But the floor was not the only option. He kissed the tip of her nose. 'Come.' He led her to the corner where a couple of sofas were stored one on top of the other. He lifted one clear and pulled off the holland cover, which kept the fabric free of dust. He set the candle on the floor beside it. 'Your *chaise*, madam,' he said, giving a flourishing bow.

She giggled.

He blinked. Never once had he heard her giggle. He laughed, swept her up in his arms and laid her prone on the cushions. He stripped off his coat and waistcoat and stretched out beside her. He cupped her cheek in his hand. 'Now, where were we?'

'Mmm...' she said. 'Either I was kissing you, or you were kissing me.'

'Why, my dear,' he said, smiling down into those pretty green eyes, 'I think—no, I distinctly remember—the kissing was mutual.'

She sighed as their lips melded together.

Chapter Ten

The reverence with which Jack touched her was almost too gentle. Yet that gentleness was what had given her the courage to return his kisses with fervour. The feel of his big warm hands wandering her hip and her thigh as he lay alongside her was lovely. Her skin seemed to tingle along the trail left by his hand as he petted and stroked her from hip to knee while his lips and tongue wooed her mouth with such care she could scarcely breathe for the pleasure it sent streaking down to her core.

Her insides tightened. She had the strangest feeling that her body might snap in two, the tension was so great. Too much to bear, yet somehow not enough. Was this supposed to happen while kissing? Neville had not been much of a one for kissing. Preferring to *get on with the task*, as he had said when he came to her bed. To her, it had been a necessary evil. Also to him, she had thought, because it had happened so rarely and usually only when he was in his cups after a night of carousing with his friends.

With Jack it was different. Magical. Enchanting.

How could she not have known this was possible? Well, she had thought it might be. For others.

She had believed her husband when he said she wasn't attractive. That her red hair was enough to kill a man's passion and that he was doing his best. She had felt ugly and ridiculous when he had winced at the sight of her naked. After that, she had always worn her nightgown to bed. And he had only come to her in the pitch dark, so he would not have to see her, she had presumed. His pinches and slaps had been equally humiliating.

'Marguerite,' Jack said.

He was staring down at her. The candlelight flickering across his face made his features stand out, though the expression in his eyes was hidden by darkness. Had she made him angry? She shivered. Always she had made Neville angry.

'Is something wrong?' he asked, running his fingertip along her jaw. 'If you do not want this, you must tell me, sweetheart.'

Sweetheart. How lovely that sounded. How large it made her heart grow in her chest. Those few kind words were like balm to her soul.

'Everything is perfect,' she said, smoothing his hair back from his face. 'Perfectly wonderfully lovely.'

The frown did not leave his forehead. She smoothed it with her thumbs. 'You have made me happy,' she said. 'For the first time in a long time. It surprised me, that is all.'

He smiled at her explanation. 'I am glad to hear that. Very glad.'

He bent his head and kissed her. The stroking began anew. And her skirts inched higher and higher with each pass of his hand, until she was trembling with anticipation of what was to come. And for once, she was certain it would not hurt.

Jack would never cause her physical pain. The re-alisation was freeing. She parted her thighs and Jack pressed his knee between them. She parted them more and soon he had wedged himself in the cradle of her hips. He kissed her lips, then slid down her body. Startled, she watched him back up, until he was kneeling between her ankles. He pushed her skirts upwards. In preparation for his entry, she assumed. But when he reached for the candlestick she gasped.

And when he lifted it high to look at her... Down there... She shut her eyes tight. 'What are you doing?'

'Admiring the view. And it is spectacular.'

She giggled. And then wanted to stuff her hand-kerchief in her mouth. Oh, he would think her so wicked. Excitement rippled through her. What did it matter what he thought? She was a widow. Free to do as she pleased, provided she did not cause a scandal. Free to discover what other women's chatter had indicated for them was an enjoyable experience.

What if he, too, found her cold, the way Neville had? Passionless, he had called her, when he bedded her the first time and it had been extremely painful. Worse was his scorn and derogatory remarks, both in their bed and out of it. It was why she had left London and stayed in the country. That and knowing he had shown all his friends those horrible pictures. If only she hadn't been so stupid as to sign them. The idea of it being published and passed around the whole of England...

Jack was staring at her, his head tipped on one side. 'There you go again, my dear. Off somewhere else and quite frankly looking quite terrified.'

Here she was letting Neville make her life miserable. Again. She could do this. 'I just didn't expect—' She waved a hand in his direction. 'I have never—'

Regret filled his expression. He set the candle aside and moved forward, returning to his earlier position, resting on his hands and looking down into her face. 'Oh, my darling girl, I am sorry. It is years since I have had a beautiful woman in my arms.' He closed his eyes briefly. 'I got carried away. I am moving too fast. I made assumptions, you being a widow and all.' He gave her a wickedly boyish smile.

He smoothed her hair back from her face. 'I should not have done that. Tell me what it is that *you* like.'

'I—' She was either going to lie, or she was going to open herself to ridicule.

No. Not true. Jack was nothing like Neville. He would not deliberately try to make her feel small. She closed her eyes, so she would not see his reaction to what she must tell him. If he left, in disgust or disappointment, she would not watch him walk away. Perhaps then it would not hurt so much.

She took a deep breath. 'My husband and I came

together but rarely. Somehow things did not go well between us. I found his attentions painful. He found me cold.' Humiliation was a hot tide in her veins.

Jack frowned. 'He hurt you?' The gruffness in his voice gave her pause. He was angry.

She winced. 'He said he was trying to warm me up, but it seemed to make things worse.' She had always hated the way he slapped her and pinched her, it was why she had vowed to remain a widow.

'I see.' Now he sounded grim.

Oh, dear, she should have said nothing. Just done what she had always done, held still and hoped for the best. Perhaps it would not hurt with Jack.

She dared to peek at his face. He was looking at her with kindness and there was a light of determination in his gaze. He gave her a gentle smile. 'I think we need to start again.'

She stared at him blankly, but then he leaned down and gently kissed her lips. 'You are, to all intents and purposes, a virgin,' he murmured against her mouth. 'And it will be my very great pleasure to teach you the way of it.' And he kissed her again. Deliciously. Expertly. Until she felt lovely and desired and warm all over.

When his hand came to her breast she stilled, expecting a painful pinch.

'Easy,' he murmured. Slowly he caressed her breast as if it was something precious. First one, then the other. They felt heavy and full and the tips seemed to tingle.

He circled her nipple with his thumb while he

continued his lazy exploration of her mouth with his tongue. Her core tightened. Her body relaxed. Oh, yes, she liked this, very much.

Jack knew some men liked inflicting pain. And he was experienced enough to know some women enjoyed being the recipients of those sort of activities. He could not understand it himself. He was all about giving and receiving mutual pleasure. Mutual was the key. Clearly this woman had not found her husband's preferences pleasing. No wonder she was so reserved.

Or had been.

Right now, she was kissing him back with delightful eagerness and her hips were arching upwards, seeking a pleasure she probably wasn't fully aware of. Her body knew. But her mind did not. When he had brought her up here to find the kite, he hadn't been bent on seduction, though he had to admit his own body had been ready the moment he knocked on her door and saw her deliciously ready for bed.

A half-truth. His body had been ready for days. He'd been having trouble focusing on his work because she had been intruding on his thoughts so much. But he had never had any trouble maintaining control of that part of his anatomy. At least, not since he'd reached adulthood.

Now, he wasn't so sure. He had been desiring her for days. And her apparent willingness to indulge him now left him at the very edge of his control. But understanding that she had suffered at the hands of her husband made him all the more determined to give her pleasure, even at the expense of his own.

Her eagerness as he touched her in her most sensual places, her unbridled excitement, had him breathing so hard he was panting and trembling with the effort of holding back.

He slowly broke their kiss and cruised his lips across her cheek to her ear. He blew softly and she shivered. 'Oh,' she gasped. 'That felt lovely.'

His shaft hardened. He rocked gently against her hip, allowing himself a fraction of the pleasure he wanted. He licked and nibbled his way from her ear, across her throat to the shadowy valley between her breasts. He felt her stiffen. Fear of pain.

He pretended not to notice and circled his tongue on the creamy flesh above her breasts while gently moulding the other breast with his palm, stroking and lightly squeezing until he felt her once more respond to the pleasure of his touch.

The heat of her mons seared his thigh. When he had viewed her quim by candlelight, the sight of the dark red curls already gleaming with the welcoming dampness of her body, the image seared his brain, but she was not ready for that sort of love play. He wanted to make her happy, not frighten her to death.

Her happiness, her pleasure, was important. Deeply important. More so than any of his casual sexual encounters. He'd had one or two since his wife died, but none of those women had touched him as deeply as Marguerite.

He groaned softly. What was it about this woman?

Was it her kindness to his children, or the aura of sadness he sensed in her appealing to his streak of chivalry? Whatever it was, he needed to make this perfect. He licked his way to her nipple, now a tight little nub beneath the cotton of her nightgown. He toyed with it with his tongue through the fabric. Her little cries of pleasure and her fast, shallow breathing were torment to his demanding cock. He ignored its wants and focused only on what brought her pleasure.

He raised his head to assure himself he was on the right track. Her expression was soft, her eyelids at half-mast, her gaze hazy and her cheeks flushed. 'Don't stop,' she gasped.

Ah, there was the other part of this woman. The independent lass who knew what she wanted. The woman who hid the vulnerable girl who had been hurt, but to whom he hoped to prove not all men were beasts.

'Your wish is my command,' he said, stealing a kiss from those luscious lips that issued orders.

She arched upwards beneath him, offering her breast to his mouth. He blew on the sensitive peak. She shuddered. 'Jack,' she moaned.

He pushed her gown upwards, until her breasts were bared to his gaze. 'Beautiful,' he murmured. Full and round and pale as the moon. The tips so light in colour as to be almost rosy. He licked first one, then the other and her hips wriggled beneath him, making his balls tighten in anticipation. Grimly, he ignored the urge. He closed his mouth lightly around the peak of her breast and circled her nipple with his tongue.

She moaned.

Gently, lightly, he suckled, giving her time to become accustomed to the pulling sensation. A small hand cupped the back of his head. The other stroked his buttocks through his dressing gown. This sign of boldness delighted him. He held still, suckling lightly while she ran her fingers through his hair and squeezed his bottom in a way that suggested she had never done such a thing before.

She traced the outline of his hip and up his spine, her touch so feathery and light it was torture of the sweetest kind.

He increased the suction on her breast and pressed his thigh harder against her mons. Her groan of pleasure made him smile and he let his hand wander down her body, until it reached the apex of her thighs. He rolled on to his hip and gently stroked one finger along her slit, so hot and wet he yearned to be inside her, seated to the hilt. Not yet. Not this time. He could not take the risk of scaring her off. First, she had to know what she was missing.

He gently played with the little nub that would bring her fulfilment, rubbing and circling with his thumb, while he slowly dipped first one finger, then a second inside the silky soft heat of her channel. He curled his forefinger against the wall, seeking—

She cried out. He suckled harder, pressing against her clitoris, while strumming that little place inside her...

Her hips came up. She screamed loud enough to wake the dead, then collapsed against the cushions, her face full of wonder. Panting and round-eyed, she stared at him. 'That was…'

'A surprise,' he teased, feeling surprisingly pleased given an arousal that was destined to go unsated.

'Much, much more than that,' she said between shallow breaths. 'Lovely. Extraordinary.'

He kissed the tip of her nose, lay down beside her and pulled her into the curve of his arm. 'Rest, now,' he murmured. 'You deserve it.'

He forced himself not to think about his aching cods. He'd deal with them later. He wanted nothing to spoil this moment.

He lay still, listening to her breathing return to normal and feeling her heartbeat slow. He felt a deep sense of satisfaction. More satisfaction than he would have expected given he hadn't reached his own climax. Which was strange, to say the least.

Her husband must have been all kinds of an idiot if he hadn't seen what a beautiful and passionate woman he had for a wife. Any man would be proud to be her husband. Independent-minded or not.

He frowned.

He supposed he wouldn't mind a little bit of independence in a wife, as long as she didn't go behind his back. Which led him to the question…did Marguerite really not want a husband?

'Good heavens,' she said, lifting her head.

He relaxed his hold on her, a little. 'Awake, are you?'

'Oh, my word. How much time has passed?'

He smothered a smile at her anxiety, but he also understood. What had happened just now had come as a shock. She would need time to understand and recover. 'A few minutes only.'

She shifted in his arms and he released his hold. 'I think I should go back to my room. In case anyone notices I am gone.'

'I cannot think who would notice.' He didn't keep his footmen hanging about in the halls in the middle of the night, the way his father had. Nevertheless, he sat up and helped her to do the same. 'Let us take the kite with us so it is ready for the morning. I will have the other toys brought down tomorrow.'

'The kite. Yes. The kite. Of course. If anyone asks, it is our reason for being here.'

'Indeed.' He pushed to his feet, straightened his dressing gown, turning his back to give her time to sort herself out.

When he turned back she was once more covered from head to toe and looking very prim and proper except for her flowing locks, which she was madly trying to braid. 'Let me help you with that.'

Surprised, she ceased her efforts. 'You know how?'

He tried not to look smug. 'I was married, you know.'

She dropped her hands and let him work. The silkiness of her hair was enough to make him want to kiss her again. He'd forgotten the pleasure of these intimate acts with a woman one cared about. Not forgotten, but pushed the memories aside. He'd been so angry. Felt so betrayed. Perhaps it was time to let the past go.

He quickly plaited the heavy mass until it looked neat and tidy. Then he turned her towards him. He tightened the belt at her waist for good measure.

'Thank you,' she said. 'My hands feel as if they are too heavy for my arms.'

Yes, she had fallen apart very nicely. 'You will feel more yourself in the morning.'

He picked up the kite and escorted her back to her chamber.

He would feel more himself when he had some time alone with his good right hand.

Chapter Eleven

Feel more herself in the morning? When Marguerite awoke at first light, she had never felt so different. She had never felt so womanly or so…so…light-hearted. She wasn't cold or without passion. No, indeed. The disaster in her marriage had been her husband.

She went about the rest of her morning in a bit of a fog. She set the girls to practising their letters, while her mind kept returning to the extraordinary occurrence of the night before. What had happened last night must not happen again. It went against everything she had promised herself. Did it not?

She frowned. Why? Why must it not happen again? What harm would it do? Besides, while she had enjoyed it enormously, what had happened had been rather one-sided. He had given her a wonderful gift, but she knew there ought to have been more. The bliss she had experienced had not been mutual. It should have been, if it was done properly. She had been so shocked she had scurried away like a frightened mouse.

Oh, no, what was she thinking now? That she needed to rectify the omission? Really? Was that her excuse for wanting to do it again? She went hot all over.

Oh, no. She needed to be sensible. Besides, how could she ever face Jack and not blush thinking about what he had seen, what they had done? She put her hands to her hot cheeks in a futile effort to cool them.

Face him she must, at dinner every day. She felt the urge to run home, to hide.

She gazed at the two little heads bent over their slates, Elizabeth with her creased brow and Janey with her little pink tongue poking out and moving as if it, too, traced the letter. So sweet. She had not yet told them of the plan for the afternoon. They would never settle to their lessons if they knew there was a special treat in store. She had to remain at Bedwell until the new governess came, for their sakes.

She glanced out of the window. It was not quite as windy as it had been the day before, but there was still enough of a breeze to get the kite aloft. She hoped.

Bother. When she saw Jack again, she would simply have to pretend that nothing had happened in case anyone noticed a difference in her. Or in his attitude towards her. She must be as she always was, no matter how strange she felt inside.

The clock struck noon.

'Tidy up, ladies,' she said.

'I'm starving,' Elizabeth said, putting her slate inside her desk and letting the lid fall with a bang. 'I wonder what is for lunch.'

'Pea soup,' Janey said. The little girl loved pea soup.

'We had pea soup yesterday,' Elizabeth said.

'I hope we have it today.'

Marguerite checked that everything was put away properly. 'Run along to the nursery and find out.'

Now that things were running smoothly in the nursery, she ate luncheon in her own room. It was a brief respite from her duties that she treasured.

The girls dashed off. They always did everything at a run. She loved their enthusiasm. She really was going to feel the loss when she returned home. She was also going to miss Jack terribly.

A tray for one was waiting on the table in her little sitting room. She lifted the covers—there was soup. Potato with leeks from the delicious smell wafting up. Poor Janey. She smiled. The little girl would live on pea soup if she was permitted. There were also cold slices of beef and ham, fresh crusty bread with cheese and pickles, and an orange.

She also was starving, she realised. She had wolfed down her breakfast, too. She could not recall her appetite being so huge before. If this was what doing that… She pushed the thought aside and tucked into her meal. She glanced at the newspaper that had been left beside the tray, but found herself unable to concentrate.

Last night had been simply too wonderful for words. At least, it had for her. What if he had been disappointed?

He hadn't seemed to mind that he hadn't found his own pleasure. Whenever Neville had not given

her his seed, he'd stomped away and told her she was hopeless.

Surely Jack would not have kissed her so sweetly or plaited her hair or smiled in quite that way if he had been dissatisfied? Or was he being too much of a gentleman to show his disappointment? Had he, too, left her side feeling somehow cheated? The joy of earlier faded.

Instead, she felt foolish.

The idea of facing him now loomed unpleasantly before her. The thought of seeing disappointment, perhaps even disgust, in his eyes made her shrivel inside.

She straightened her shoulders. Face him she must. Appetite gone, she folded her napkin and placed it on the tray. She might as well get it over with. She marched down to the nursery.

The girls were finished with their lunch and the table had been cleared. They were now sitting cross-legged on the floor, building something out of bricks. No sign of Jack. He must be too busy to visit today. Strangely, there was no sign of the kite against the wall beside the nursery door, where they had left it last night.

He must have thought better of letting them fly it and had it removed. Blast it. Why could he not see how good that sort of thing would be for his children? What would it matter if they skinned a knee or banged an elbow in the process? The experience would make them stronger and nimbler.

Alfred, the footman, appeared at the door. 'His Lordship is waiting in the front hall, my lady. He

said to ask you to come down if you and the Ladies Elizabeth and Jane are finished with lunch.'

Surprised, she stared at him. Marguerite's heart tumbled over, causing her the oddest little pang. Joy. Happiness. How did he make her feel this way with such a normal request?

She swallowed. She must keep him at a distance. Protect her foolish heart. She was not such an idiot as to think last night would have the same importance for him. Men liked their pleasures. It was as simple as that.

'Quickly, girls,' she said. 'It will not do to keep your father waiting.'

Elizabeth looked puzzled. 'Papa is coming on our walk this afternoon?'

'It would seem so,' Marguerite said, trying not to grin and give things away.

'Hooray,' Janey shouted and tugged at her coat until it fell down from the hook and smothered her in its folds. She struggled free.

Marguerite laughed. Elizabeth giggled and Janey looked highly pleased with herself. In short order and with help from Lucy, they got their coats on and hurried downstairs.

'There you are at last,' he said as they ran down the last flight of stairs into the great hall. 'I was beginning to think you had decided you preferred to stay in the nursery.'

Janey pointed to the kite he was unsuccessfully trying to hide behind his back. 'What is that?'

'It is a kite,' Elizabeth said. 'I saw a picture of one in my book. *K* is for kite.'

'A kite,' Janey squealed and jumped up and down. 'What does it do?'

Jack grinned. 'It flies. Come on, I will show you.'

'Do I have to sit on it?' Janey asked, taking his hand. She sounded intrigued and a little nervous.

'No,' Jack said and swung her up on to his shoulders. 'You have to sit on me.' She squealed with delight and drummed her heels on his chest. He captured her little boots in one large hand. 'Careful. Never kick a willing horse.'

'My turn,' Elizabeth said, reaching up.

'It will be your turn on the way back,' Jack promised.

They trooped outside on to the lawn.

It took a bit of time to initiate the girls into the secrets of kite-flying, but Jack was patient and the girls eager, so after a half-hour or so, with first Elizabeth on the end of the string and then Janey taking a turn, the kite lifted high overhead and danced and dipped in the breeze. Marguerite's role had been to run with each girl while Jack tossed the kite upwards. Now she stood back and watched Jack show his daughters how to control the darting red diamond. When to pull it in and when to run and when to let the string play out.

The wind scoured the children's cheeks until they were rosy. Their eyes shone with joy. Marguerite wanted to hug them, she felt so happy for them. She wanted to hug their papa, too, as he romped with his little girls. The upswell of emotion shook her to the core of her being. Her eyes watered. It must be the wind. She sniffed and dashed the moisture away with her glove.

'Look at me, Lady Marguerite,' Janey called out since it was her turn now. 'I am flying.'

Indeed, she looked so tiny on the end of the long string, Marguerite could imagine the kite lifting her and taking her away.

Jack grabbed the string higher up and gave it a few swift tugs as the kite showed signs of drifting downwards.

Elizabeth left her sibling and father and came to stand beside Marguerite. 'I have never seen Papa so happy,' she said, her little face a picture of ancient wisdom. 'He never played with us before. Thank you.'

Surprised, Marguerite stared at her. 'This was all your papa's idea. There is nothing to thank me for.'

Elizabeth smiled knowingly up at her. 'He hardly ever visited the nursery before you came. And he never ever let us go outside.' The kite began to do cartwheels. 'Janey,' she shouted. 'Don't let it fall. It is my turn.' Off she ran.

Marguerite gazed at Jack. Yes, he had changed. So had she. And the eldest of his girls had noticed. She winced, recalling her own childhood. She had noticed a great deal more than people thought in those days, too.

She and Jack were going to have to have a talk.

After such an eventful afternoon, Marguerite had brought the girls back to the nursery and left them to quieter pursuits while she went to work on the very last of her drawings. A very rare orchid found only in the wildest of places. The outdoor air seemed to have invigorated her spirit and the work went very well indeed, so it was with a cheerful heart she returned to her suite to dress for dinner.

Nell had laid out her best gown, the blue one Marguerite had bought when she was in London visiting her brother. She frowned. 'That is not the gown I usually wear to dinner.' She wasn't quite sure why she had brought it, to be honest. It had been more a matter of habit than a plan to wear it.

The girl's pale face flushed. 'I beg your pardon, my lady. I thought that with the vicar coming to dinner... I will fetch the other one.'

Marguerite's stomach rolled. 'His Lordship never mentioned he was having guests to dine?'

The maid gathered up the gown. 'Reverend Purvis dines with His Lordship on the first Thursday of every month, my lady. They are both single gentlemen and, as I understand it, they like a bit of company. Mayhap His Lordship forgot to mention it.'

Should she dine with the two men or take her meal in her room? Would it look odd if she hid herself away? Or would it be worse if she joined them? Likely it was better to stick to the usual routine. Because no matter that she would prefer her governess adventure not get to her family's ears until she was ready to tell them, she wasn't foolish enough to have it reach them smacking of something clandestine. Which it surely would if she tried to hide her presence in His Lordship's household. If she was going to come to the vicar's attention, she was going to meet him properly.

She smiled. 'That gown will do very well, then, thank you, Nell.'

Nell beamed. It didn't take them long to get her into the gown. 'May I do your hair, my lady?' the maid asked. 'I saw this lovely hairstyle in a copy of *The Lady's Monthly Museum* that I would like to try my hand at. I am sure it would suit you. If I am to become a ladies' maid, I will need the practice.'

The longing in the girl's voice was palpable. And Marguerite could not fault her for being ambitious. 'Very well, you may try, but if I do not like it, you must promise me you will take it out and pin it the usual way.'

'I promise, my lady.'

Marguerite sat down at the dressing table. Instead of feeling impatient, as she did, she should be pleased at the luxury of having a maid do her hair as a lady of her rank would normally expect.

After half an hour Nell stood back to admire her handiwork. 'What do you think, my lady?'

The style was elegant yet feminine and attractive. Perhaps it even made her look younger.

Her heart picked up speed. Would Lord Compton like this new version of herself? Good lord. Hopefully he would not get the wrong impression and think she had improved her appearance for his sake and was throwing out lures. 'I do like it,' she said to Nell and hopefully managed to keep the doubts out of her voice.

The young woman beamed. 'Thank you, my lady.' She glanced at the clock. 'It is time you went down. His Lordship will be in the drawing room with the vicar.'

'You think the vicar will have arrived by now?'

'Oh, yes, my lady. Mr Laughton says you can set your watch by the vicar's arrival time. Always here at half past the hour.'

And dinner would be served at seven, so in just a very few minutes. 'Very well. I will go down at once.'

Jack had forgotten all about the blasted vicar coming for dinner until his valet had reminded him while he was dressing. And, yes, it really was the first Thursday in April. April already. The weeks were flying by. Before long he'd be planning for the harvest. And he hadn't yet found a permanent governess for his girls. His mood dipped. It was another of those tasks he did not relish. Not the least because it would mean Marguerite would leave. He forced himself to focus on his guest, instead of thinking about the woman who had brightened his days and his nights.

'How do you find your flock, Vicar?' he asked, as he always did. 'This rain must have been exceedingly tiresome for you while making your rounds.'

The vicar was a scholarly, serious-looking man who peered at one as if he was short-sighted and was trying to see right into your soul. 'I have been dodging the showers, to be sure. Quite a few of my older parishioners are complaining of rheumatism.'

Jack nodded. 'As has Nanny James.' To his great chagrin. He should have seen it long before now.

'How is the planting coming along?' the vicar asked.

'The rain is slowing us down.'

Purvis nodded wisely. 'Let us hope we have seen the last of it.'

The door opened to admit Lady Marguerite. For a moment, Jack couldn't speak. She always looked attractive, but tonight she seemed to shine. The gown was a pale blue and had clearly been made by a skilled modiste. While not extravagantly low across the neck, it was low enough to reveal the creamy skin of her throat and offer an intriguing glimpse of the valley between her shapely breasts. A valley he had become intimately familiar with the previous evening. The skirt belled out at the hem, revealing a pair of nicely turned ankles and feet encased in satin slippers the same colour as the gown. A festoon of some white gauzy stuff caught up by bunches of yellow silk roses completed the picture of an elegant noblewoman. She had done him proud.

His gaze caught hers and her green eyes flashed a challenge. Did she expect him to comment in surprise? Why would he be surprised at her beauty? He had seen it from the first.

Catching himself, he moved forward to greet her, holding out his hand, which she bestowed upon him with great aplomb. 'Lady Marguerite, may I present the Reverend Purvis, our vicar?'

She dipped a little curtsy and held out her hand. 'A pleasure, Reverend Purvis.'

Reverend Purvis's cheeks flushed pink. 'Dr Walker did mention—'

Jack raised an eyebrow. 'I am sorry, Vicar, I neglected to mention that Lady Marguerite would be joining us for dinner.' He really hadn't been sure she would come down. 'Lady Marguerite has kindly agreed to give me pointers about the management of the children, now Nanny James is no longer fit for the task. I am deeply in her debt.'

The Reverend Purvis took her hand and bowed. 'My lady,' he murmured. 'I believe that while we have not met I have heard your name mentioned upon a few occasions. You reside in Westram, do you not?'

She nodded briskly. 'I do, indeed. And shall be returning there as soon as Lord Compton has found a suitable governess for his daughters. Sadly, while I did not have children before my husband died, I gained a great deal of experience helping my father bring up my siblings.'

'It is good of you,' mumbled Purvis, clearly overawed by her graciousness.

'It is, indeed,' Jack agreed, noticing how neatly she had introduced the information of her widowed state and her expertise. He noticed that she did not mention she was being paid as an interim governess. Nor should she. It was none of Reverend Purvis's business.'

'May I offer you a glass of sherry, Lady Marguerite?' Since the first night they had eaten together, he had always simply ordered her ratafia, but tonight with a guest present the circumstances required he act the perfect host.

'Thank you, Lord Compton.'

He tried not to show his surprise at her acceptance of an intoxicant. Was she in need of Dutch courage? He narrowed his gaze on the vicar. One out-of-place word and he—

He repressed the overwhelming urge to protect Marguerite. Firstly, any sign of such a reaction would not serve her well and secondly the lady was quite able to protect herself. However, he would hold himself ready, in case he was needed.

The footman poured her a glass and brought it over. He and the vicar raised their glasses. 'To your very good health.'

She nodded her acceptance and took a delicate sip. Oh, yes, when she wished, Lady Marguerite could play the grand lady and no one would mistake her for anything other than a member of the aristocracy. Pride at her competence and her *savoir faire* made him smile. She really was an extraordinary sort of woman.

He was going to miss her when she returned to her cottage. The sense of loss that thought engendered came as no surprise. It wasn't the first time he'd thought of her departure with regret. The thing was, might there be an alternative?

'Lady Marguerite, your family hails from the north, does it not?' asked the vicar.

'The Greystokes have inhabited Gloucestershire

for a hundred years or more, but we are originally from Kent.'

'Kent? Really?' said Purvis.

Lady Marguerite's green eyes twinkled mischievously. 'From this very house, in fact.'

Jack hadn't been sure that she knew her family had once owned this estate. He hadn't liked to bring it up in case there was remaining resentment. It seemed she only found the coincidence amusing.

Purvis frowned. 'The Greystokes owned Bedwell?'

'Before the Commonwealth tossed them out. Of course, it was not called Bedwell then.'

The vicar's lips pinched. 'Cromwell. A disgraceful fellow.'

'Oh, I don't know, Vicar,' Jack said. 'He wasn't all bad. You have to admit the Stuarts were no angels.'

'I cannot say they did not deserve some sort of restraint, my lord, however, I believe the methods were barbaric.'

'Cromwell proved to be no better than the Stuarts in the end, in my opinion,' Lady Marguerite said. 'The Lord Protector seemed to lose sight of his principles once he became all powerful.'

'I agree, Lady Marguerite,' said the vicar. He sounded most surprised.

'From the diaries existing from those times, it is clear my family began to feel the same way,' Jack said. 'They were among the first to welcome back King Charles the Second, once he agreed to the terms offered.'

'Hence their retention of Bedwell,' Lady Marguerite said, smiling. 'Our family took a while to work their way back into favour.'

'My uncle resides in Gloucestershire,' said the vicar. 'You may know of him. Captain Trim. A naval man originally, he retired to Tewkesbury.'

'The name is not familiar. My brother's estate is south of there, near Chedworth.'

The vicar nodded. 'Well, now that Uncle Trim is a Member of Parliament, he moves in more exalted circles than I. No doubt he knows Lord Westram. I shall write to tell him of the pleasant evening we spent together.'

Lady Marguerite nodded and smiled, but Jack sensed her disquiet. Oh, good Lord, do not say she was keeping her whereabouts a secret from her family? That would not do at all. It was his wife's deceitful behaviour that had led to her death. This was something they would need to discuss.

'Does your family hail from Gloucestershire, Vicar?' Jack asked.

'Dear me, no,' said Purvis. 'I was raised in Suffolk.'

Though she tried to hide it, Lady Marguerite looked relieved. Yes, she was definitely keeping secrets. He should have known better than to have trusted her word that her family approved of what she was doing. Disappointment swamped his earlier feelings of well-being. He hated the idea she might have lied.

He hated lies.

Chapter Twelve

Thank goodness Jack had found a new topic of interest for the vicar. Even so, every now and then, Marguerite felt Jack's searching gaze on her face. She pretended to notice nothing, but it seemed he had sensed something not quite right about her replies.

The man had taken her aback when he had talked of relatives in Gloucestershire. With her luck, she might have known that the one person invited to dine with Lord Compton would be the only person in Kent with an uncle who lived near her brother and who likely knew him.

There was no help for it but to write to Red and tell him that she had taken a temporary position in Lord Compton's household with stress on the word *temporary*. She would also have to tell him that she needed the money and tell him to mind his own business.

Not that it would likely do any good. So, the sooner Jack found a replacement governess the better.

'Suffolk is not a county with which I have much personal knowledge,' she said.

'Most gentlemen think of Newmarket when they think of Suffolk,' Lord Compton said. 'One of the best racecourses in the country.'

'It is true,' the vicar said, 'though my family prefers the raising of livestock to racing it.'

Lord Compton chuckled.

Marguerite breathed a sigh of relief. The comparison of pedigrees and family roots had been successfully got over.

'Well, it looks as if we are finally done with Bonaparte,' Lord Compton observed.

'I was astonished that he actually abdicated,' Marguerite said. 'From Emperor to commoner.'

'Indeed, yes,' Jack said. 'I am also relieved the government was not foolish enough to accept his attempt to have his crown passed on to his son.'

'A clear ploy to continue to rule,' Marguerite said. 'Lord Liverpool clearly saw through it, along with our allies. I for one am so glad the tyrant is finally dealt with and we can have peace again.'

'It is a wonderful thing,' the reverend agreed. 'It is time all those young brave men returned home.' The vicar looked guilty. 'I beg your pardon, Lady Marguerite, I understand that your husband was lost in the war.'

'He was,' she said. She found herself unable to say more. After all, one did not express one's thankfulness at a person's demise, even if in one's heart one saw it as divine intervention.

Fortunately, the men had finished their desserts.

'It seems it is time for me to withdraw and leave you gentlemen to your port and your discussion of politics. No doubt you will have all England's problems solved before the end of the evening.'

They rose as she stood. She dipped a slight curtsy. 'I will bid you good evening, gentlemen. It was very pleasant to meet you, Reverend Purvis. I hope our paths will cross again.'

The vicar bowed. 'Indeed, Lady Marguerite, the pleasure was all mine.'

A footman opened the door for her to pass through and she hurried upstairs. As a general rule, the lady of the house would take tea in the drawing room, where the gentlemen would join her after they had finished imbibing their port, but since she was not Lord Compton's wife or his hostess, she could make her escape.

Upstairs, she checked on the children in the nursery. Lucy glanced up from her mending with a smile. 'The children are sleeping, my lady.'

'Excellent,' Marguerite said and retired to her own chamber. She seated herself at the writing desk to compose her letter to Red. Bother the minister. But this really was the only thing she could do. And when Red insisted she returned to live under his roof, what then?

Well, she would deal with that problem when it arose.

The next day, Marguerite was hard at work finishing the drawing of the orchid, when a knock sounded on her door. She started. Everyone knew to leave her in peace for the last few hours of the afternoon. 'Come.'

It was Alfred. 'Lord Compton requests your presence in his study, my lady. If you would be so good?'

She frowned. She had half-expected Jack to come to her last night, after the vicar left, but since she did not hear the sounds of his departure until well after midnight, she was not surprised when Jack did not appear. Likely he was too far gone in his cups to do anything except fall into bed.

Still, she had been in a fever of anticipation and it had taken her hours to fall asleep. Which was very foolish of her. Her happiness did not depend on the whims of any person and especially not those of a man.

'Please inform His Lordship I will be there shortly.'

The footman bowed and left.

Marguerite removed her work apron, looked regretfully at her easel and made her way to Jack's study.

He was standing at the window when she entered. 'You wanted to see me, my lord?'

He turned to face her. His brow was lowered, his gaze dark. 'You led me to believe your family knew what you were doing here, yet last night I had the distinct impression you were not happy that the Reverend Purvis would relay your whereabouts to your brother.'

It sounded like an accusation. And as if he thought ill of her. 'I believe I said that my family were aware of my independent state and had no say in what I do or do not do.'

'While I do not recall the exact words of our conversation, you intimated that they knew you were hiring yourself out.'

'They know I earn money from my drawings.'

'But this is more than that. This is working as a governess. I cannot approve—'

'No, you cannot.' She glared at him.

He blinked. 'I cannot…'

Heat rose upwards from her chest. 'You have no right to approve of anything I do or do not do. You practically begged me to take this position. Talk about look a gift horse in the mouth. If you do not want me here, all you have to do is say so.'

'I didn't say I didn't—' He took a deep breath as if trying to rein in his temper. Marguerite's heart picked up speed. Panic filled her.

'Of course I want you here,' he said, 'or I would not have asked you. I do not like the idea of you deceiving your family.'

She clenched her hands together, trying to calm her fear. Jack wouldn't lash out at her the way Neville had. She was sure of it. 'You are right. I did not tell Westram that I was acting as interim governess. However, I wrote to him last night to inform him of my change of circumstances. The letter should have gone out with the mail this morning.'

His mouth thinned. 'I did not frank a letter for you.'

A spurt of anger flashed up from her chest. 'Are you saying you do not believe me?'

His eyes widened. 'Is there a reason I should not believe you?' He took a deep breath. 'I beg your pardon, I am simply concerned. I merely meant I could have saved you an unnecessary expense.'

Yes, that would be like Jack, to consider saving her an expense. She should not have jumped down his throat or thought the worst, even if he was thinking the worst of her. 'I did not think of it, quite honestly. I gave Laughton the money for the stamp.'

'I see. Well, I am glad we have that settled.'

'Yes. I am glad, too.' She had started to forget how controlling he was, how rigid his rules. 'Have you had any replies to your advertisement for a governess?'

He winced. 'I have. It was my main reason for asking to see you this afternoon.'

His main reason had been to haul her over the coals. She forced herself past her irritation. This was what she wanted, was it not? For him to find a replacement and for her to get back to her life. 'You wished me to look at them?'

An odd expression crossed his face. Regret? Well, she felt regretful, too. The thought of leaving this house and returning to her cottage suddenly seemed daunting. And lonely. She was so fond of the children. Something she had never expected.

But she was also becoming far too fond of their father. And while he had introduced her to the most amazing thing she had ever experienced, with both gentleness and kindness, it was the other side of him that she feared. The controlling side.

The side of him that didn't believe her when she said she had mailed a letter to her brother as if he did not trust her. Neville had been similarly controlling. He had not let her visit her family or see them alone.

Yes, there were things about Jack Vincent that scared her, even now she knew him better. For one thing, she still had not discovered why Lizzie had appeared so panicked by his threat of a fate worse than death.

'The applications are on the table by the window,' he said, gesturing. 'I thought we might look through them together before my bailiff arrives.' He glanced at the clock. 'He's due here in an hour.'

He flashed her a smile that was so charming yet so unassuming, her heart tumbled over. Was that his intent? To make her forget that just moments ago he had been behaving as if she had committed some sort of crime? Well, she was not going to forget. Or be fooled by that smile. She didn't dare.

Neville had always apologised after he struck her, always said it was her fault. That she made him lose his temper and that it would not happen again. It always happened again. No, she did not intend to permit any man to have that sort of power over her life.

She sat down in front of the pile of papers, picked up the top one and glanced at it. 'How many are there?'

'A half-dozen, at least.'

'Let us hope there are some good ones among

them.' Then she could go home. Again, sadness welled up.

'You think we will find more than one to be suitable?'

'If so, you will have to interview them. Perhaps also have them meet Elizabeth and Janey, so you can see how the children react to them.'

He groaned. 'If it is anything like the last one, they are going to react very badly. You are the only governess they don't seem to have plagued to death, no matter how much I threaten them.'

'And what is it that you threaten them with that scares them so much?' she asked. She waited in trepidation.

He made a face. 'Their great-aunt Ermintrude. I am afraid I made her out to be some sort of disciplinarian, poor dear, and I drag her out of the closet every time I need them to behave. If they ever meet her, they will know instantly that it was all a hum. Despite the way she looks, she is completely harmless and would be of no help to me at all.'

Relief filled her. She had been unable to help worrying about the threat that had the girls looking so hangdog. She had been so afraid it was some sort of corporal punishment he had in mind. He had never shown any sign of that level of anger in his dealings with his daughters, but if you asked anyone about Neville, they would all have said he was the most charming of fellows who wouldn't hurt a fly.

He would. As long as the fly was weaker. 'Poor

lady. It is better to offer a carrot than a stick, you know.'

He looked amused rather than affronted. 'What do you mean?'

'Offer them the treat of something they like to do, in place of something you do not want them to do. Like flying the kite as against sneaking out to visit the stables.'

'Ah, horse riding. I have asked my bailiff to look for a suitable pony. Hopefully it will not take too long.'

Marguerite beamed at him. 'Then you can use riding lessons as a carrot for good behaviour.'

He grinned. 'I understand your point.'

He sat down next to her on the sofa and pushed the papers around as if he didn't want to start looking at them. 'Were you disappointed that you did not have children with your husband?'

The very idea made her go cold. 'I was never so pleased about anything in my life.'

He looked startled.

'As I mentioned before, I brought up my siblings. Enough was enough. I prefer to concentrate on my drawings.'

'And yet you say you are not a good artist?'

Trust him to spot the flaw in her argument.

'It is my independence I value. I care nothing for recognition.'

'I see.'

Did he? Most men did not understand a woman's desire to be free of male domination. They assumed a female could not manage alone, despite the many examples all around them of women doing exactly that. 'Shall we look at the applications?'

He frowned at her change of topic. 'I suppose we must.'

'Were there any here that you particularly liked the look of?'

'I have not had a chance to look at them yet.'

'Then we shall have to start from scratch.' She scanned the first one. 'It might help us if we had a sheet of paper and listed the attributes we like and those we don't as we go through each one.'

'Good idea.'

He got up and went to the desk while she read the letter a little more carefully.

After a moment or two, she became aware that he had not returned with paper and pen, and glanced up. He was staring at her with longing in his gaze. And heat.

Her body warmed. Her breasts tingled and there was an odd tightness in her core. All that from a glance? Was this his real reason for him asking her to come to see him this afternoon? A repeat of the other night. Excitement rushed in a hot tide through her veins.

It was if she was two different people. A strong independent woman who earned her own living and the woman who melted at the first sign of this man's desire. Was it because she had never before known the storm of sensation he had fired up in her? It had certainly taken her by surprise and she had been dreaming of experiencing it again.

Heat rushed to her face at the direction of her wicked thoughts. 'Is something wrong?'

He seemed to come to himself with a start. 'Nothing at all.'

He picked up the items she had requested and returned to sit beside her. He was a big man. And she could feel his warmth along her side and her every breath took in his scent. A lovely manly woodsy scent. She tried not to breathe it in. It made her feel dizzy and even hotter.

Governesses. They were here to choose her replacement. Concentrate.

She stared down at the letter. 'Our first applicant is Miss Louisa Shepherd. Write her name down,' she directed. 'And draw a line across the page and about three lines down, then we can compare apples and apples. She is forty-five and seems to have about fifteen years' experience as a governess and—' she riffled through the pages '—four referees. We will look at those more closely when we have been through all the applications once. Four households seems about right, don't you think? Not too many in fifteen years, but enough to give her plenty of experience.'

He wrote down forty-five and fifteen in one column and four employers in another.

'She was educated at Bakewell Academy.'

He wrote that down.

'She teaches needlework, reading, writing and geography, but recommends a tutor for mathematics since it is not her forte.'

'Needlework, English, no mathematics,' he repeated as he wrote.

Oh, dear, this was going to take a very long time indeed. Perhaps she should have asked him to wait until later, so she could at least get some work done today. No. It was better to get this over with as soon as possible. She was already feeling terrible about leaving, she did not want to drag it on any longer than necessary. Besides, she had no doubt that Red would be coming to see her very soon and talking about her causing a scandal and badgering her to return home. To his home.

What would he say if he knew she had managed to have two scandals hanging over her head?

At least she nearly had all the money she needed to deal with the worst of them.

Chapter Thirteen

Jack was so hungry it was a hollow ache low in his gut. But not for food. He wanted the woman going through the letter from some spinster governess or other that he'd likely be stuck with for the next ten years.

Watching her go through the applications, he wanted to tip up her chin and taste the pretty lips that were talking of years of service and other such stuff. Or he might, like some naughty youth flirting with his first maiden, enjoy stealing a couple of pins from her hair in the hope of seeing that glorious auburn mane of hers tumble down around her shoulders.

And if she'd decided to rap his knuckles with her ruler, it would have been totally worth the pain. But she wouldn't. He could see from the colour in her cheeks and the sultry cast of her mouth she, too, was thinking about kissing.

Only he had decided that taking advantage of her while she was still in his employ and living under his roof was not a gentlemanly thing to do. He'd already done it once. He was not going to do it again.

All this uncontrolled lusting after a woman was beneath him. He was a peer of the realm and a magistrate to boot.

'This one is barely out of the schoolroom herself,' she said. 'I do not think we should consider her at all.'

He dragged his gaze from her lips to stare at the letter. 'She does say she speaks fluent French.'

'Hmm… So did one of the others.' She took his list and ran her finger down the items spread across the page. 'This one here.'

Lord, but she would make a good wife.

A perfect wife.

If she wasn't so dead set on her independence.

That sort of woman would not do for him at all. He wanted a wife who would listen to and obey her husband in all things. No. Marguerite would not make him a good wife, but heaven help him, he would love to nibble on that dear little ear and run his tongue—

'Jack?' she said, her voice husky.

He lifted his gaze from the delicate line of her throat. The longing in her eyes made him nearly swallow his tongue. 'Marguerite?'

Her fingertips grazed his cheek for the briefest moment. 'You were staring at my ear.'

'And your throat and the lovely curve of your cheek and the way your eyelashes look against the light.' Good God, what sort of drivel was coming out of his mouth? He sounded like some idiot schoolboy.

Her eyes widened. 'Jack. That is the loveliest thing anyone has ever said to me.'

He wanted to preen. 'It is all true,' he said gruffly. 'Devil take it, I am going to miss you when you leave. I have not enjoyed myself so much for years the way I did yesterday with the girls. Last night at dinner with the vicar, your presence made all the difference.' She had filled a gap he had not known existed. He was going to miss her like the very devil.

Perhaps once she had returned to her own domain, they might conduct a discreet affair... His body hardened.

Her gaze softened. 'I will miss you, too. And the girls.'

The words touched him so deeply they tugged at something inside his chest and caused it to ache there, too.

She gave him a shy little glance, leaned forward and pressed her lips to his, a soft quick brush of silky warmth that sent blood coursing wildly through his veins.

Before he knew it, he had cupped her nape and was holding her in place, returning her kiss. And then they were kissing, their tongues tangling and their breaths mingling and rasping in his ears.

He slowly eased her backwards until she was prone beneath him. He raised his gaze and looked down into her face. Her green eyes sparkled, her cheeks glowed and her lips parted in a smile. 'Well, Jack,' she said quietly, almost gravely. 'It seems we both know exactly what we want.'

* * *

The weight of Jack's large body pressing Marguerite into the sofa cushions was delicious and despite that her hands were trapped between them she did not feel in any way confined or restricted. Perhaps because she bore only a fraction of that weight, a mere hint of it, as he supported himself on his hands and gazed down into her face.

The heat in those lovely blue eyes seemed to scorch her face. Yet he did not fall on her like a wolf upon prey.

'Are you sure?' he asked.

There was such longing in his voice and such loneliness in his eyes she wanted to offer comfort. Perhaps even to offer to stay, after the way he had talked about missing her.

But he was a man who liked to control all around him. He would make rules. Demand obedience. Her heart fluttered madly as if wanting to flee. Recollections from the past reared their ugly heads. The pain and humiliation inflicted by the man who was supposed to honour and protect her loomed large. Her boldness of mere seconds ago shattered into fragments.

No. Not once had Jack treated her with anything less than respect. Indeed, he had not taken his own pleasure while giving her the wonderful gift of learning that she was as passionate as any other woman. He deserved she give him something in return, if indeed that was something he wanted? His kisses made her think he did, but… 'When you did not come to me last night, I wasn't sure—'

'I did. I stood outside your door for a good five minutes.' He laughed ruefully. 'But hearing no sound, I decided it was too late.'

'If I had known, I would have stomped around the room and made all kinds of noise.

They both laughed at her silliness.

He leaned down and kissed the tip of her nose. 'Then let us not have any misunderstandings tonight.'

She swallowed.

He gave her a quizzical look. 'Unless you have changed your mind.'

'No,' she said. She snatched at a fragment of bold-ness and clung to it like a lifeline, forcing herself to smile up at the gorgeously handsome man peer-ing down at her with a puzzled frown. 'I have not changed my mind.'

He looked unconvinced as if he sensed her trepi-dation. 'Then you come to me.'

'What?'

'Come to my chamber tonight, if you are still of the same mind. Come at midnight. I will be waiting, but I shall leave the decision to you.'

She stared at him blankly. This man who liked to control things was leaving matters in her hands? She took a deep breath. 'Very well.' If she could pluck up the courage.

The clock struck the quarter-hour.

'Oh, my goodness, your bailiff will be here at any moment.' She pushed at him and he sat back and helped her to sit up. She patted at her hair, pleased to discover it tidy, though no doubt her face was as pink as a peony.

She picked up the list they had been working on and handed it to him. 'I would choose number three if I were you.'

'I will write to her at once.'

Heart pounding, she fled from the study.

For the rest of the afternoon, Marguerite could not focus. The precision on which she prided herself simply was not there. The roots looked stiff and awkward. The petals would not curve. The stamens were far too large. She tore up the second sheet of paper.

All she could see in her mind's eye was Jack's face. The gentle smile. The gleam in his eye. The way the lock of hair drooped over one eyebrow when he leaned over her.

Her breast tingled in a most shocking way every time she recalled the feel of his hand resting there. And he had left it to her to decide whether or not to go to him tonight. She would go. Soon a new governess would be hired and she would go home. There would be no more dalliance. No more Jack.

A sense of loss rose like a tight little lump in her throat. Then she must make the best of the time she had.

A knock came at the door.

She almost jumped out of her skin.

'Come?'

'A note for you, my lady,' Alfred said.

Marguerite's stomach fell away in a rush at the sight of the handwriting on the note. She took it with a smile and closed the door, staring down at the note. It had been hand-delivered.

She broke the seal. Read the bold, flowing words.

Your month is almost up. You cannot hide from me. I saw your advertisement in the post office. Mr Barker was most helpful in letting me know that another gentleman had already enquired about your services as a drawing teacher.

Damn. She should have taken the notice down. Blast Barker and his gossipy ways. Not that she hadn't intended to keep her appointment. She had. She simply did not like the idea of that horrid man following her to Bedwell.

The letter continued with a great many underlinings for emphasis.

I will take a payment of five pounds as a show of good faith. Meet me tomorrow night at Bedwell's gate.

Her heart thudded wildly. Five pounds? She rushed to her desk and unlocked the desk where she kept her wages. Five pounds would eat a hole in the sum she had been saving. But, yes, she could manage it and still have enough for the final payment after she received her wages from Jack at the end of the week. It would also be an opportunity to inform her blackmailer of her determination that the next payment would be the last. If she did not get the picture back, she would redraw it and publish it herself for the money she would earn from it and be damned to him.

She felt ill. The idea of ruining her family name in such a way was not to be borne. They would likely hate her for ever. And rightly so. But hopefully such an unscrupulous man would not guess that she would never follow through on such a threat. Because if he did, then she might find herself paying him for the rest of her life. Or having to confess the whole affair to Red. She wasn't sure which was worse.

Feeling ill, she tucked the note in the drawer. Her hands shook as she locked it. She closed her eyes. Perhaps she should talk to Jack about this. He was a magistrate. He might be able to help.

He'd be shocked. Probably disgusted that he had allowed a woman like her to associate with his children.

The thought of him looking at her with revulsion caused her heart to ache.

No. She could handle this by herself.

Marguerite's gaze flew to the clock. It was almost five. The thought of facing Jack over dinner, of making conversation while they both knew what they had planned for later, made her heart seem to rise in her throat. Excitement. Hope. Fear.

She could not face him and speak with any kind of normalcy. She would send word down to Laughton that she would take a tray in her room this evening. And after that she would make her final decision about whether or not she would go to Jack.

Chapter Fourteen

She would come, Jack thought, swirling the brandy in his glass. She might have forgone dinner with him, but she had courage, his Marguerite, and if she said she would come to him, then she would.

Midnight came and went.

Perhaps he had made a mistake in leaving matters in her hands. She had been so bold this afternoon, so sure of herself, of her desire for him, it had pleased him to think she would take the initiative. He tossed back the wine. If she did not arrive in the next five minutes...

The door creaked open.

He rose to his feet and smiled at the vision in bare feet with her tumble of wild curls flowing around her shoulders and her dressing gown primly belted. He opened his arms. She walked into them and he held her close.

She buried her face in his dressing gown and he could feel the rapid beat of her heart against her chest. 'I was sure someone would see me.'

He chuckled, delighted by her arrival and by her obvious embarrassment. He tipped up her chin so he could look into her eyes and pressed a swift kiss to her lips.

'Everyone is abed by this time, sweet.'

'Do not be too sure. There is always someone stirring because they need the chamber pot or a warm glass of milk.'

He laughed out loud. 'Not tonight apparently.'

She smiled. 'No. Not tonight.'

'I missed you at dinner.'

'I could not have eaten a bite knowing...' She swept out an arm, encompassing his chamber.

'Would you like brandy?'

She nodded.

He poured her a glass of brandy and topped up his own. When she would have sat down on the sofa, he swung her about and pulled her on to his lap in the large armchair.

She giggled.

'I have been looking forward to kissing you again all afternoon and evening,' he said brushing her hair back from her face, 'so do not think you are going to keep me at a distance.'

'I have no wish to keep you at a distance,' she said, sounding breathless.

'Good.'

She bent her head and kissed his lips, her tongue lightly flicking against his and driving him wild with desire. Her hands caressed his shoulders, his nape, ran through his hair and finally cupped his cheeks with a tenderness that was endearing and lovely.

To his regret, she broke the kiss and gazed into his eyes. 'You have turned me into some sort of wanton, Jack Vincent.'

He thought of how severe she had seemed outwardly, yet how passionate she had been about his girls at their first meeting, ordering him about and taking him to task.

'Oh, I don't know,' he said. 'I think the wanton has always been there. I just helped release it from its cage.'

She stilled, staring down at him, her lips parted, her eyes catching the firelight.

'I am sorry,' he said, lightly, puzzled by her reaction. 'I am teasing. I intended no insult.'

She blinked slowly, as if coming back to herself. 'None taken. Indeed, I believe you are right.'

Since the idea seemed to please her, he let the matter go and drew her head down to once more plunder her lovely mouth while he buried his hands in the mass of hair that fell around them. He loved her hair.

He loved her lips, her touch, her fiery blushes. He also loved her razor-sharp mind. Perhaps he was wrong about her not being the right sort of wife for him. The thought of making Marguerite his and having access to these kisses and not having to go sneaking around in the middle of the night was both startling and exceedingly tempting.

As long as he set out the rules and the reasons

for them right from the beginning, it might work. Might it not?

Although, she had said she didn't want children and he needed an heir. On the other hand, what woman really did not want children of her own? It would be something they would have to talk about.

Right now, what he wanted was her in his bed. He rose to his feet. She gave a small shriek and broke their kiss. 'You might give a person a bit of warning.'

He pressed a kiss to the top of her head. 'Do not tell me you thought I was going to make love to you on a chair when there is a lovely soft mattress nearby? If you do, I shall not believe you, my lady.' He carried her into his chamber, where he earlier had made things ready.

His lady. He would really like her to be his lady. But those sorts of discussions would come later. He laid her on his bed and gazed down at her while he let his dressing gown fall to the floor.

He was as aroused as he had ever been in his life. He'd been aroused almost constantly since her arrival under his roof, though until tonight he'd mostly had it under control. Now he wanted her to see just how much he desired her.

She gasped and ran her gaze down his length, lingering on his erection before returning her gaze to his face. She gave him a cheeky grin. 'I have a feeling you are proud of that.'

He chuckled at her display of courage, because he could also hear the trepidation in her voice, no matter how hard she tried to hide it. 'I have been told it is impressive.' He cocked an eyebrow, wondering what she would say next.

Her smile was as much shy as it was bold. 'I will take your word for it.'

So, endearing. Nothing like the courtesans he'd become used to, more like a new bride still feeling her way around the marriage bed, which was a little odd since she'd been married for years. He brushed the thought aside and joined her on the bed, laying alongside her. 'Your turn.'

'My turn?' She looked puzzled.

He loosened the knot of her gown and then moved his hand away, intrigued as to what she might do next.

'Oh,' she said. She hesitated, then, drawing in a breath, untied the belt and let the dark blue wool fall open, revealing—

He sat up to get a better look. It was the most erotic, daring nightgown he had ever seen. The fabric was a pale blue wisp of stuff that fell just above her knees with lace in strategic places. He touched one of the lacy bits on her chest and it parted to reveal her nipple already hard and begging for his lips and his tongue.

His body tightened.

She giggled and made a movement with her hand as if she would cover herself, but then stilled, gazing up at him with a naughty smile. 'I am told men like this sort of thing.'

'Oh, I like it,' he said, exploring another of the lacy openings. Another beaded nipple came into view and then, at the apex of her thighs, he glimpsed the tight red curls that had filled every salacious dream he'd had of her.

'I like it a great deal.' He inserted first one finger, then another into that lacy opening and stroked her hot wet slit until her hips arched upwards, then he bent and took one hard little nipple in his mouth and toyed with it with his tongue.

She gasped and moaned and writhed with pleasure at his touch, but when he came over her, she stilled. Only for a second. A mere fraction of a moment, but he felt as though he had been struck by a blow to the heart.

Instinctively, she had expected pain.

He rolled on his back.

She came up on her elbow, looking anxious. 'I am sorry, I—'

He lifted her so she was straddling his hips and smiled up at her. 'Show me what you like, my sweet.'

'Oh, but I—' An expression of understanding dawned on her face. She leaned forward, compressing his cock and causing him exquisite pain. She pressed her lips to his in a brief swift silken touch, then she sat back on her heels to regard his swollen shaft.

The smile she gave that stupid piece of his anatomy almost made him lose control. He never lost control. Not ever.

'Please,' he said, shocked by the rasp in his voice.

With the smile of a satisfied cat, she rose up on

her knees and took him inside in a long slow slide of discovery.

He gripped the sheets in his hands. He could do this. He could let her set the pace. He hoped.

Marguerite knew exactly how this worked. For once in her life she was glad of her trips to the barn where the milkmaid and the dairyman indulged their passion.

The bird's-eye view she'd had of them had been an education. The first time, she'd gone there with the idea of sketching the view from the loft window, but the sounds below had drawn her attention. The couple had regular trysts when they thought they were alone.

Thinking about what they did had always made her warm all over. Neville had questioned her unmercifully about the accuracy of those sketches. Asking her how she had learned of such things if she had not participated herself. He'd made it seem sordid and lewd. The reactions of his friends had reinforced his mockery. She'd been highly relieved when he'd finally stopped showing them around.

Was it because he had lost it? Was that why it had fallen into the hands of her blackmailer?

Jack, on the other hand, seemed thoroughly delighted with this way of making love. Or was he?

He seemed a little tense, the sheets fisted in his hands as if his life depended on it.

She hesitated. He opened his eyes. 'Please. Do not stop.'

Amazingly, he had relinquished control. A thrill of desire zipped along her veins. The sensual expression on his face encouraged her to continue her exploration of the amazingly lovely feel of him deep inside her.

She rocked back and forth and the place where their bodies joined tightened with delicious pleasure.

The faster she moved, the more pleasurable it felt. He lifted his hips in counterpoint to her movements and slid deeper. It felt so good. She ran her hands over his chest and across the breadth of his shoulders.

He groaned.

Her heart seemed to grow inside her chest as if that sound of pleasure was the source of great joy. She leaned forward to kiss his lips and the change of position caused extraordinary sensations. 'Oh, my word,' she gasped, coming upright.

He opened one eye and gave her a naughty smile. 'Oh, yes, sweetheart. Experiment. Try riding me like a horse. See how that feels.'

At her blank glance, his smiled broadened. 'Like posting for a trot.'

She lifted up and sat back down, his member sliding within her. The growing tension inside her made it difficult to breathe or to think.

And when he put his hands on her breasts and fondled them gently, the amazing thing that had happened before crashed over her.

'Marguerite,' he said in a harsh exclamation. 'I'm—' She reached the crest and slid over the top.

Hot bliss rushed outwards.

He lifted her and she collapsed on his chest, aware of him moving beneath her for a moment or two. A guttural groan rose up from his chest and his body went lax.

They lay panting, their breaths mingling, her heart racing so hard she was sure he must hear it. He reached over and pulled the sheet across her, settling her more comfortably in the crook of his arm with her cheek against his shoulder.

'That was…' she said vaguely.

'Yes,' he murmured. 'It really was.'

She drifted into sleep.

Marguerite wasn't sure how long she slept, but it was still dark when she opened her eyes and clearly Jack was awake. He twisted a lock of her hair around his finger, then let it spring free in a little curl. He did it again.

She tilted her head and kissed his chin, the stubble of his chin rough against her lips.

'Awake already?' he whispered. There was a smile in his voice. It made her feel warm and comfortable.

'More or less.'

He shifted and gave her a long lingering kiss.

She put her arms around his shoulders and kissed him back. 'Thank you.'

He chuckled. 'No, no, my lady. Thank you.'

'I did it right?'

'You did it perfectly.'

The anxiety still niggling at the back of her mind stilled. She really had. Done it perfectly. 'It was lovely.'

'Yes. Perfectly lovely.'

She heaved a sigh of happiness. She wasn't cold. She had simply been unlucky in her marriage. 'I should return to my room.'

'I am afraid so. It is nearly four. I will walk you back.'

'No need. Indeed, it would be better if you did not.'

He helped her off the bed. He ran his hands down her shoulders and arms and took her hands in his, stepping back to admire her. 'I love this nightgown of yours.'

Oh, she had enjoyed wearing it for him. 'I am glad you approved.'

'It is a shame to cover it up.' He held up her dressing gown and she slipped her arms into it and stood still as he tied the belt.

Then he drew her into his arms and held her close, kissing her deeply. 'Until next time, my sweet.'

She slipped out of the door and made it back to her room without seeing anyone.

The next day, a storm had rolled through in the early morning, leaving the sky a leaden grey in its aftermath.

She had sent a note to Jack, letting him know she was indisposed for the day, and after dressing she had lain on her bed, knowing her nemesis would not care how ill she was and he would expect her to keep the appointment later that evening.

When Mrs York brought her dinner tray along

with a tisane, she managed to sit up and eat the soup, but the rest was beyond her.

She sent the tray away and sat in the chair with her eyes closed. She could do this. She must. Marguerite wrung out a cloth and placed the cold compress across her forehead. She had been forced to cancel the girls' lessons for the day because of her headache. Although the rain had now ceased, the headache was a low thrum at her temples, likely caused by the knowledge of her upcoming meeting.

At the appointed hour, she forced herself to put on her cloak and slipped down the servants' stairs. She was glad when she did not run into anyone. She used the side door that led to the stables and then cut across the edge of the lawn to the drive.

A prickle across the back of her neck caused her to whip around quickly. Her head spun. She closed her eyes until she was steady. There was no one there. It was her imagination, her guilt.

The air was cool on her skin and smelled of spring, of growing things and clean fresh rain. She inhaled a deep breath and forced herself to stroll calmly to the gate and out into the lane.

The faint smell of cigar smoke and the small point of glowing of red gave the man's location away. She approached slowly. He was standing close to the hedge a little way from the gatehouse. She could see little more than a dark shadow.

'You are late,' he said.

'I am here now.'

'Do you have my money?'

'I do.'

A gloved hand shot out, palm up.

'Be warned,' she said. 'The next payment will be the last.' She fumbled for the purse inside her reticule.

'I told you it would.' His voice was sullen and she did not believe it for a moment.

'I mean it. I will publish it myself, if you ask for one penny more.'

'You wouldn't dare,' he sneered in that oddly familiar way that struck a faint chord in her memory. A painful chord.

'Who are you?' she asked.

'Someone who wishes you well.'

'Liar.'

He chuckled. She knew that laugh. Somewhere she had heard that laugh before. If only she could place it.

He counted the money she had given him. 'Well done, Yer Ladyship.'

Now he had changed his voice. Made it sound rough. Like a Londoner. Why would he do that? He must be someone she knew. One of Neville's friends? One of those who had smirked at her drawing?

He grabbed her arm and pulled her close. He was wearing a mask. Why would he do that if she did not know him? She tried to see his eyes, but it was too dark.

'One week from today, I want full payment.' He closed his hand around her wrist so hard it hurt.

She cried out with pain. She tried to twist free,

but he was too strong. 'You will have your money when I am back in Westram, as arranged,' she said through the pain of his grip.

He glanced up and down the lane. 'Eight sharp. Behind the Green Man as before. Do not fail.'

He pushed her and she stumbled away.

She rubbed at her arm. 'I will be there, but mark my words well—it is the last payment I make to you.'

He walked away as she was speaking. She did not know whether he had heard her or not.

Mouth dry, heart racing, she hurried back to the drive and the safety of Bedwell. Who was he? Why did that voice seem familiar? Why could she not remember?

He'd spoken in a whisper before, in the church and in the alley behind the Green Man, likely in case he was overheard. Here there was no one to hear him and he had let her hear his real voice.

'Lady Marguerite.'

A shadow loomed in front of her, large and menacing.

Startled, she halted, with a gasp. Then she realised who it was. 'Jack? I—'

'Out for a stroll, I see.' His tone was dry.

She swallowed. 'I— Yes. I needed fresh air after being cooped up all day.'

'Your headache is better, then?'

Her head was pounding. But there was a note of disbelief in his voice. 'Much better, thank you. What are you doing out here?'

'Keeping an eye on you. I saw you leave the house and was concerned for your safety.'

Her heart stilled. Had he seen— 'As you can see, I am quite safe.'

'Are you returning to the house? May I escort you?'

The urge to tell him what was happening, to unburden herself to him, was almost overwhelming. But the thought of what he would think of her when he knew the truth blocked the words that wanted to tumble out. He was a magistrate. A man who liked rules and order. He would be appalled to know about the sort of trouble she was in. Just as Red would be appalled.

No, she did not want him to think of her that way. Not after the wonderful moments they had shared. Besides, with a new governess in the offing, their liaison would soon be at an end, and she ought not to trouble him with her problems.

She just hoped she was right about the woman she had suggested. She really wanted to feel that she had left the girls in good hands. She was going to miss them so much. And Jack.

Oh, she was really going to miss Jack.

'Let us go in by the front door,' Jack said as they approached the house.

What could she say?

In the entrance hall, a surprised-looking footman took their outer garments.

'Join me for a nightcap in the library,' Jack said, tucking her arm through his, giving her no opportunity to refuse without causing some sort of scene in the hallway.

That she would never do. He did not deserve it.

She winced as he inadvertently touched the spot where the blackmailer had hurt her. He glanced down, but there was no expression on his face. She could not tell what he was thinking.

A footman followed them into the library, but Jack waved him off. 'I can manage, thank you.' He saw her seated and then brought her a brandy.

She sniffed at it and then put it aside. 'Strong drink will not help my headache, I am afraid.'

He frowned. 'If you indeed have a headache.'

She stiffened. 'What do you mean.'

'I saw you meet that man in the lane. Saw you kiss him.' He sounded disgruntled.

She stared at him in shock. He thought she had kissed... How dare he?

'I did not kiss him.'

His frown deepened. 'I know what I saw. I also saw you give him money. Why else would you sneak out of the house in the middle of the night, if not to meet another of your lovers? I have to say it is extraordinarily clever of you to take money from one lover to give to another.'

Anger rose in a hot red tide. 'My God. What sort of person do you take me for? If you did not go creeping around at night poking your nose—'

She stopped herself. He clearly didn't trust her— why should she bother to be upset by his accusations?

She turned her face away so he would not see how badly his accusations hurt. 'Think what you wish.'

He made a sound like a growl. 'I have to think what I wish when you will not tell me what is going on. I have to use my own eyes and ears and come to logical conclusions.'

He sounded so…hurt. He was…jealous.

A pain pierced her heart. She had not wanted to hurt him. Never wanted to hurt him, she cared for him too much.

A lump rose in her throat. She didn't just care for him, she had fallen in love with him. She'd known it for days and had refused to admit it.

'It is not what you think,' she said. 'Yes, I gave him money, but he is not nor would he ever be my lover.'

'You owe him a debt.' His voice was flat.

She hesitated. It was as good a reason as any other and better than the truth. 'Yes.'

He paced to the console and back. 'Why are you lying?'

She risked a glance at his face. Yes, she had hurt him, but now his eyes were sharp and his expression one of puzzlement.

'You are lying,' he said. 'I can hear it in your voice. See it in your face.'

She winced. 'Only because you are asking for information that is none of your concern. Why can you not accept that?'

He sat down beside her and took her hand in his, gently, firmly. 'Because I care about you,' he murmured. 'Why will you not let anyone care for you?' His hand closed around hers and a twinge from her wrist made her flinch.

He pushed up her sleeve. The skin was red and already beginning to darken. He glanced up at her face, his eyes full of anger. 'He did that to you? Damn him. I won't have anyone hurting a woman under my protection. Who is he?'

She put her hand over his, felt the warmth in that big hand and felt the slight tremble that spoke of the anger running beneath the surface. 'Please. Do not concern yourself. It was a misunderstanding.' She pulled her hand free of his and he let it go. He did not try to hold her fast against her will and for that she was grateful.

'You know I can find out who he is for myself.'

She stared at him. 'How?'

'I doubt it will take me long. As a magistrate, I have access to all sorts of information about people who enter and leave this Parish.'

He spoke with such confidence, she believed him. This could be the answer. If she knew who this man was, maybe she could put a stop to his demands. Permanently. Because for all her brave words to that horrible man, she would never willingly publish that drawing.

Why would she not trust him? Jack stared at her, saw the longing in her eyes, the battle going on behind her fearful expression.

What was it about him that the women he cared

for most in the world did not trust him with their secrets? Was it him?

This man, whoever he was, had hurt her. Why would she keep his identity hidden if he was not a lover? Or perhaps he was a relative. It was certainly someone she cared about more than she cared about Jack.

Oh, that was a stupid thought. He wasn't jealous. He was simply trying to get to the truth. And to help her, because she seemed so distraught. She had nigh on fainted when he had spoken to her on the drive.

'You could really find out who he is?'

Was that a hopeful note in her voice? 'I can and I will, if you do not give me his name.'

She shook her head. 'I cannot.'

Because she did not trust him. He wanted to hit something.

She took a deep breath and something in her expression cleared. She actually looked relieved as if he had lifted some sort of burden from her shoulders. She was going to tell him after all. He'd seen such relief before when questioning those accused of some petty crime. The need to tell someone what they had done. Not that she would fall into that category. But the look was the same.

She gave him a quick hesitant glance and looked away.

His stomach dipped. Whatever she was going to tell him, it was not going to be good.

'The man I met out there in the lane approached me some time ago. At my sister's wedding. He was behind me in church, so I did not see his face, but he told me he has something of mine that would cause me and my family a great deal of embarrassment if it became public.'

His jaw dropped. This he had not expected. 'He is blackmailing you?' He could not keep the shock from his voice. Or the anger. If he had known, he would have taken that bastard out there in the lane and put his fist right through his face. What a blackguard. 'Tell me who he is and I will deal with him.'

She drooped and leaned back against the sofa cushions, staring at her fingers as they twined around each other. 'That is the problem. I do not know who he is. He has never revealed his face and I believe he disguises his voice.'

He frowned. 'Then it must be someone you would recognise if you saw him.'

'Yes. I have come to that conclusion myself, though not as quickly as you.'

Hah! She thought to flatter him, did she? Well, that would not wash. She had been lying to him for weeks, not to mention that this person, this criminal, was hanging around outside his house, close to his daughters and— He stopped his racing thoughts at the sight of the sorrow on her face.

'I apologise, Jack. I should not have come here.' She shook her head slightly. 'I needed the money. I had no idea he would follow me. I am to make the final payment next week. Tonight, I threatened to deal with him another way if he asked for more money after that, but I honestly do not think I will ever be free of him. I will leave first thing in the morning.'

She had read his concerns as if he had written them down and handed them to her. But he felt her hurt like a blow to the solar plexus. He was wrong to hold her responsible, it was the man holding her hostage who was to blame.

'No. You will stay here until we get to the bottom of this.'

She stiffened. 'I think not. Up until now, he has behaved like a gentleman.' She shuddered. 'Almost. But I think he is getting desperate. I do not want him coming here again.'

'Marguerite,' he growled.

'Jack, this truly is not your concern.'

'As a magistrate, it is very much my concern.'

Her gaze shot to his face. 'Please. I do not want any sort of scandal.'

Damn it all. 'I will be discreet, I promise you.'

She winced. 'When you find out who he is, would you send a note to Westram cottage and let me decide what to do? Perhaps if I meet him this last time, he will abide by his word and leave me in peace.'

'What you will need to do is lay charges.'

Her soft green eyes widened. 'But that would mean a trial and—'

'What the hell does he have that causes you to fear him so much?'

She met his gaze full on and he saw her brace for his reaction. 'It is a series of salacious sketches on a single sheet of paper. Cartoons, if you will, depicting the Prince and Mrs Fitzherbert doing what people do in the privacy of their bedrooms.' She winced. 'In great detail.'

He gave her a blank look. 'What on earth does that have to do with you?' Understanding dawned. 'You drew them.'

She nodded. 'I drew them and I signed them when I was still in the schoolroom. My father was always talking about the Prince, how he despised him and his philandering and I guess he sparked my imagination after I saw them together when we visited London. The images do not flatter the couple, especially not the Prince. I should have burned it. When Neville, my husband, found it in my portfolio he showed the sketch to some of his closest friends.'

Good lord. Of all the political disasters for her brother that one was a fine one. 'One of them took them?'

She nodded. 'I have come to believe so. Tonight, I thought his voice sounded familiar, but he only spoke a few words and I simply could not place him.'

'We will find out who he is and get them back. He will not receive another penny.'

She looked unconvinced. 'Even if we knew who he is, how can I force him to give up the picture? Oh, I really would prefer not to have Red embarrassed in this way.'

'Leave this blackguard to me.'

'No. This is not your problem, it is mine. What if he drags you into it and you are embroiled in the scandal? Think of your daughters.'

The thought gave him pause. Given the Prince's strange starts, the man could just as easily blame Jack as he would blame the Westrams. Guilty by association. Damn it all.

She put her small hand on his, the long artistic fingers so pale and white against his own skin. 'It is all right, Jack. This is not your problem. I will deal with it. I beg you not to concern yourself. Indeed, I would prefer that you would not. I will leave first thing in the morning as I said.'

Damn it all, she was refusing to let him help her at all, because no doubt she had seen his hesitation when it came to his girls. He could not help but admire her selflessness in putting his daughters before her own interests.

'I insist—'

'No, Jack. I will not allow it.'

Devil take it. He could not force her to do his bidding. He had no right to offer her his protection. They were lovers. Nothing more. And she was another woman who would not put her problems into his hands and let him deal with them.

And in that case, there was nothing more to be said. 'Very well. Go if you must. And I will find out who he is and let you know. At least, let me do that much for you. Exactly how much time do I have?'

Gratitude shone in her eyes. 'The meeting is set for a week from tonight. I am to meet him behind the Green Man. Promise you will not take any action without talking to me first. Please, Jack.'

And with that pleading look in her gaze, she tied

his hands. He clenched them into fists. 'You should talk to your brother about this. It is his right to know what is going on and to see to your safety.'

'I would prefer not to put this burden on his shoulders. Once I know who it is, if I discover I cannot deal with him myself, then I will go to Red. I promise'

It was the best he could hope for. 'Very well.'

She rose to her feet. 'Now you really must excuse me. I am tired and I need to rest if I am to depart in the morning.'

Damn it to hell. He was going to miss her like the devil and so would the girls, but it was for the best. For them both. Wasn't it? If she didn't trust him, how could he ever trust her?

Chapter Fifteen

'That is everything, my lady?' Mrs York said, looking at the small trunk in the middle of Marguerite's sitting room. The sitting room that would soon be the domain of the new governess.

'Yes, thank you, Mrs York.'

She and Nell had spent the morning packing.

'We will miss you at Bedwell,' Mrs York said. 'The house has been a happier place since you arrived.'

Marguerite stared at the woman in astonishment.

Mrs York blushed. 'I have not seen the master so happy as he has been these last few weeks. Likely because his daughters are happy.'

'I am glad to have helped. I am sure Lady Elizabeth and Lady Jane will be just as happy with their new governess.' She did not address the question of Jack's happiness. It was not her concern. Though he had looked decidedly unhappy last night when she told him about the blackmailer.

And so he should. She had brought her trouble with her to his home when he had been so good and kind and generous. She glanced around her room one last time. She was going to miss this place. Dreadfully.

'I think it is time I said goodbye to them.'

She left Mrs York supervising the removal of the trunk. It was to be delivered to Westram later in the day, by way of a carter. She did not want the villagers seeing her arrive home in His Lordship's carriage, so she would drive herself in the trap, just as always.

When she entered the nursery, Lucy was there with the three girls and Nanny James. Jane was sitting on the horse, while Lizzie rocked her back and forth.

When Elizabeth turned her head and saw Marguerite, she left her sister's side and went to the window, staring out with her back turned.

'I came to bid you farewell,' Marguerite said, trying not to feel hurt by Lizzie's obvious dismissal.

Janey slid down off the horse and came running. 'Papa told us you were leaving. I don't want you to go.'

Marguerite picked her up. 'You knew it was only a temporary arrangement, until you got a proper governess,' she said, giving her a squeeze and inhaling the scent of soap and little girl. 'I will miss you, too, but I am sure I will see you again in the near future.' She put her down. 'So be a good girl and mind your new teacher. That will make your papa very happy.'

'I will,' Jane said.

Marguerite shook hands with Nanny James and gave Netty a kiss on her downy soft cheek. 'Look after them well,' she said around the lump in her throat.

Lucy dipped a curtsy. 'I will, my lady.'

Nanny James gave Marguerite a sharp look. 'You'll be back, mark my words. My rheumatism says so.' She rubbed her papery-skinned hands together. 'Thank you for the ointment, my lady. Made all the difference it has.'

Marguerite crossed to the window and stood behind the stiff little back that refused to acknowledge her presence.

'Will you not bid me farewell, Lady Elizabeth?' she said softly. 'We have been good friends, have we not? One does not ignore the departure of a friend, you know.'

'You are not a friend,' the little girl said, her voice husky.

'I will always be your friend,' Marguerite said firmly, 'whether you want me to be or not. And I will expect you to write to me once a week and tell me how everyone is doing here.'

The little girl spun around. 'Why? Why would I do that when you do not care enough about us to stay? Everyone I care about always leaves, because they do not care enough to stay. So why should I care to be your friend?'

Marguerite's heart ached for the little girl. 'Lizzie,' she said, softly, 'leaving does not mean a person does not care.'

'Yes, it does, or you would stay.'

The logic was faulty, but terribly sweet. 'Not everyone is leaving. Only me. Your papa is here, and Nanny James and Lucy. I have my own home and I must return there. If you write to me, I promise I will write back and tell you all my news.'

Not that she expected there would be much. Oh, she really did not want to leave these little girls who had become such a large part of her life these past few weeks. For their sake, though, it was better if she departed.

The little girl's lower lip trembled. 'I do not want you to go at all.' She burst into tears and threw her arms around Marguerite's waist. 'We all want you to stay,' she said through her sobs.

She crouched down until they were at eye level. 'Listen, Lizzie. You and I will always be friends and, when you are old enough, you can ride over to Westram and visit me. What do you think of that?'

'I can't ride.'

'But soon you will learn, I am sure.'

She wiped her eyes on the back of her hand. 'Do you think so?'

'Yes, I think so. I shouldn't be at all surprised to learn in your first letter to me that your papa has bought a pony to add to his stables.'

A smile appeared amid the tears. 'I would like that.'

'I know. But you must be a good girl and help your papa, for he has a great deal of responsibility. Indeed, you must help him all you can by making your new governess welcome. After all, you are the lady of this house, you know.'

'I am?'

'You are indeed.'

'Oh.' She thought about it for a moment or two. Her little shoulders straightened and she nodded. 'I will try.'

'Good girl.' Marguerite kissed her cheek, her heart feeling as if it might crack open at the sight of such bravery, and stood up. 'I bid you all farewell until we meet again.'

To a chorus of rather wan goodbyes she left the room.

She had not expected it to be so hard. She had not been upset when she left her father's house to get married all those years ago. She had been full of expectation and hope. Now she felt terribly sad.

She halted at the sight of Jack leaning against the wall outside the door, his arms folded across his chest. He looked grim.

'Are they all right?' he asked. 'I had hoped to make the parting easier, but they were in floods of tears when Lucy shooed me out earlier.'

Fondness for this man who cared so much for his children rose in her throat and seemed to stick there like a solid lump. She swallowed hard before she could speak.

'They are not jumping for joy,' she said. 'But they are accepting, I believe.' She remembered her words to Elizabeth. 'I did tell Lizzie you would soon be purchasing a pony for your stables.'

He started. 'Did you now?'

'I am sorry if I spoiled your surprise, but she needed something to look forward to. Do not forget that loss of riding privileges will prove to be a better threat than Great-Aunt Ermintrude and will help with the settling in of the new governess.'

He put up a hand. 'No need to say any more. I admit you are right.'

'You are a good man, Jack Vincent.'

He looked disgruntled. 'Your trap is at the door.'

She took a deep breath. 'Good.' She continued down the hallway and was surprised when he followed her.

'I will be in touch as soon as I learn anything,' he said in a low voice.

The reminder of why she was leaving made the pain inside her sharpen. 'Thank you.'

At the bottom of the stairs, he bowed. 'Thank you for your help, Lady Marguerite. I am ever in your debt.'

Unable to speak for fear she would disgrace herself, she nodded and walked out of the front door.

Marguerite was not surprised that she had heard nothing from Jack when the following Wednesday rolled around.

Likely he had been happy to wash his hands of her and his promise to discover the identity of her blackmailer merely a sop to his conscience.

No, that was unfair of her. Likely he had been unable to discover the man's identity after all. He said he would try and she trusted him enough to believe he would make every effort.

She trusted him. What a strangely comforting sensation to know that there was one man she trusted to keep his word. Unfortunately, it was that reliability, his adherence to rules, that also made her uncomfortable.

She just wished she did not miss him so much. Him and the girls. She had been thrilled to receive her first letter from Elizabeth. She really hadn't expected it. Children were notoriously bad correspondents. Her own brothers and sister, for example, hadn't written a word once she got married and left the house, despite their promises.

She had written to them, though. Most of the letters had gone unsent, because Neville had insisted he read everything before it left the house. She had been shocked when he had called her to his study to tell her that her letter to her father, a litany of misery, must be rewritten if she wanted it to go in the mail.

When she refused, he had forced her to sit at her writing desk and had dictated her letter. He had made her write to her family weekly thereafter and had reviewed every one of them. She never received any replies.

Or had she? She had never thought to ask Petra if she had written back. She had simply assumed her family had moved on with their lives and forgotten all about her. Was it possible Neville had not given her their answers?

In hindsight, she certainly wouldn't put it past him.

The letters she'd written expressing her true thoughts about her life as a married woman, she had burned as soon as they were finished. In some odd sort of way, putting those things down on paper, even if no one else ever saw them, had brought her a measure of comfort. Oh, how she had vilified Neville in those little notes to herself. He would likely have given her a good beating if he had ever seen them.

Instead, he'd left her with a blackmailer to deal with, damn him. And deal with him she would.

She'd worked hard at the last of her drawings these past few days and had sent them off. In the meantime, a payment for work she'd sent previously had arrived, so she had enough money to meet the blackmailer's demands. And once she had been paid for these last drawings, she would have enough to live on for the rest of the year.

Dread was a hollow ache in her stomach. What if he was not satisfied with what she had paid him and continued his demands?

She would be forced to carry out the threat she had made. First, though, she would need to write to Red and confess the whole before she carried out her plan to redraw the picture and send it to the newspapers anonymously.

She really hoped it would not come to that.

At four in the afternoon, in preparation for her meeting, she counted out the sum demanded and placed the coins in a small velvet bag. She ensured the pistol Ethan had given her before he left for Bath was clean and loaded and placed it in the pocket of her cloak. She could not believe it would come to that, but she had decided it was better to be safe than sorry.

When it was time to make dinner, she discovered that she had no appetite. The knowledge of the upcoming meeting was like a lead ball sitting in the middle of her chest. It left no room for food. Instead, she sat in in her chair beside the window and watched the shadows slowly lengthen, until it was time to leave for her appointment.

Walking through the village, clutching the little velvet bag in her hand, she tried her best to look as if she was on an important errand. She did not want people stopping her and engaging in conversation. She didn't dare be late. Fortunately, not too many villagers were about at this time of the evening. Most were indoors with their families or happily ensconced in the parlour of the Green Man.

The days were lengthening now that spring had arrived and the shadows were not quite as deep as they were the last time she had walked up the lane behind the Green Man.

A few yards along, the telltale scent of cigar smoke alerted her to the presence of the man she had come to meet. Last time, she had been the first to arrive. This time he was waiting for her.

'Hand it over,' he growled.

Yes, that really was a note of desperation she heard in his voice and again she had the sense of familiarity. She peered at him, but his face was hidden by a scarf up around his mouth and his hat, a workman's cap, pulled down low over his eyes. Perhaps she had been wrong after all in thinking him a gentleman.

He poured the coins out into his palm and counted them.

'It is all there,' she said tersely. 'Please give me the picture as you promised.'

'Now, why would I do that?' he said with that increasingly familiar sneer. If only she could remember…

'I'll not pay you one penny more.' Her threat sounded weak. She steadied herself. 'I mean it. I will not give you so much as a ha'penny.'

'Is that right?' He sounded amused. She wanted to hit him. She clenched her hand around the pistol in her cloak pocket, determined to make him understand.

Another figure loomed out of the gloom. For a moment she thought it must be an accomplice. Until the figure grabbed her blackmailer by the shoulder, swung him around and planted a very neat blow to his chin.

The blackmailer lay on his back, looking up at his assailant. 'Who the devil are you?'

'No,' Jack said. 'You are the devil. Now hand the picture over.'

'I don't have it.'

'Then it is off to jail for you.'

'What? No. You can't—'

'I can and I will.'

The man struggled. 'Then I will show everyone what I have.'

The identity of the blackmailer came to her in a flash. Horror and disgust roiled through her.

'You!' she said. 'How could you?'

'You know this man?' Jack asked, yanking the fellow to his feet by his coat collar.

'He is my deceased husband's youngest brother, David Saxby.'

Jack gave him a shake, then marched him over to the patch of light coming from the Green Man's window. 'Saxby, is it?' he said, glaring down into the young man's face.

David looked green about the gills. 'Unhand me,' he said, in more of a squeak than anything. 'I'll have you up on a charge of assault.'

'And I will have you charged with blackmail,' Jack said through gritted teeth. 'How will your family like that?'

'They will not like it at all, will they, David?' Marguerite said, suddenly enjoying herself. 'No doubt your grandfather will cut you off without a penny.'

Her husband's grandfather was feared by all and sundry in the Saxby family. He was the holder of the purse strings and it was he who had arranged for her and Neville to marry. He had wanted his family to go up in the world. Having one of them sent to prison for a crime would not suit him at all.

David reached into his pocket and drew out a folded sheet of paper. He flung it at Marguerite. 'Take it. I wouldn't have published it anyway,' he said sullenly. 'Why would I want my family's name associated with that sort of smut?'

Jack grunted his disapproval and gave David another shake. He looked at Marguerite. 'Is that it?'

She opened the paper. 'Yes.'

'What do you want me to do with this blackguard?'

'Nothing.' She plucked free the velvet purse David was still clutching. 'I will have this back, though.' She moved closer to her persecutor. 'I happen to like your grandfather and would not see him hurt, but know this, David Saxby—if you ever come near me or anyone in my family, I will let Lord Compton do with you as he wishes and the devil take the scandal that ensues, for I do not give a fig for it.'

'Neville always said you were a difficult bitch,' Saxby sneered. 'Had to keep you in line the hard way, he said.'

Jack put his fingers around the man's throat. 'One more word from you and you will breathe your last, do you understand?'

David nodded.

Jack pushed him away. 'Go. Get out of here before I change my mind.'

David stumbled off.

Jack put an arm around her shoulders. 'Are you all right?'

She leaned against his lovely warmth and strength. 'Thank you.' She wanted to weep out of gratitude and out of love. And kiss his dear lips. And weep on his shoulder with relief.

She did none of those things. They were friends,

nothing more, and she could not allow her feelings to make him think otherwise.

'Come, let us get you home,' he said brusquely.

The sharpness of his tone wounded her. But it was no more than she deserved.

Jack had never been so furious in his life. It was all he could do not to strangle Saxby when he had had his hands on the blackguard. If it were not for the fact that he sensed Marguerite was on the brink of collapse, he might have done so and devil take the consequences.

His arm about her shoulders, he swept her along, half-carrying her, half-walking her. Well, he might not have murdered David Saxby, but he was damned if the bastard was going to get off scot-free. Jack was going to have a word with this grandfather of his at the first opportunity.

When they reached the cottage, he took the key from Marguerite's shaking hand, opened the door and escorted her inside.

The place was just as chilly as he remembered. The scent of tallow candles pervaded the place. And no wonder, if she had been giving all her money to that damned blackguard Saxby.

'Sit,' he commanded.

She flinched.

Damn. 'Please, sit down, my dear. Let me get you something to fortify your spirits.' He looked about him. Would a widow living in such straitened circumstances have anything stronger than water or milk?

She ceased untying the strings of her bonnet to wave in the direction of the corner beside the hearth. 'There is some sherry in the cabinet.'

Sherry was better than nothing.

He poured them both a glass. When he saw how her hand still shook, he put the glass down on a side table, undid the strings of her bonnet and tossed it on the chair on the other side of the room.

He then folded her fingers around the glass and brought it to her lips. 'Drink. You will feel better.'

She laughed shakily and took a sip. 'My word, my lord, you are in a rage, are you not?'

Beneath the brave words and smile there was a lingering fear. It dawned on him that she might think his anger was directed at her. The idea left him with a cold feeling in the pit of his stomach.

'I apologise for my harshness. I must say, it is a good thing you were present or I might have strangled the little weasel.'

She relaxed. A little. 'Weasel. The perfect description. I was on the cusp of recognising his voice when you arrived. If I had blurted out that I knew him, I don't know what he might have done.'

The cold feeling spread. A man as desperate as Saxby might have done the unthinkable. 'What the hell were you thinking of meeting him alone? I asked you to wait until you heard from me.'

'I could not. If I had not arrived at the appointed time, he would have published the sketches. I could not let him do that without one more try to appease him. For my family's sake.'

Damn it. Did the woman never think of herself? 'He might have killed you once he realised the golden goose had laid its last egg. What would your family have thought then? I can tell you from experience it is none too pleasant.'

'Oh, Jack. I am sorry. I know what happened to your wife, but I was not unprepared.' She showed him her pistol.

He made a face of distaste. 'I am sorry, but that little pop would scarcely make a dent in a kitten, never mind bring down a fully-grown man. Indeed, if you want my opinion—'

She opened her mouth.

He touched a finger to her soft lips, felt her breath against his skin and closed his eyes briefly. This was not about his feelings, it was about her safety. 'If you want my opinion, which I know you do not, but you are going to get it anyway, waving a pistol like this about is likely to get *you* killed. Not your assailant.'

Her eyes rounded. 'I do know how to use it.'

He shook his head. 'Have you ever killed any-thing?'

'No. But my father insisted I learn how to shoot when I was a girl.'

As he had suspected. 'Shooting at a target is not the same as shooting a person.' He let go a breath, tried to ease the tightness in his chest. 'But I am glad to see you went prepared.'

She took another sip of her sherry. The colour

began returning to her face. 'You are right,' she said. 'I am not sure I would have had the courage to shoot him.'

'You do not lack courage, my dear. Not in the least. But I am glad I arrived in time to put a stop to his preying on you. I don't think you will have any further trouble with him, but I will speak to his grandfather, because he has obviously got himself into debt and is desperate. Who knows what sort of foolish thing he will think of next.'

'His grandfather will likely disown him.'

'It would serve him right.'

Her hand was steadier now, she looked calmer. He wanted to take her in his arms and hold her, to assure himself she was safe. She wouldn't appreciate it, he was sure.

She put her drink down and hung her head. 'I expect you want to see what it was that I was so anxious to have returned.'

He hated to see her so beaten down. He wanted to strangle Saxby all over again. He recalled the triumphant words he'd overheard. *'Had to keep you in line, the hard way.'* Clearly, bullying ran in the Saxby family. He could only imagine what Marguerite had suffered at the hands of her husband. 'Not unless you want me to.'

She looked surprised and relieved. 'It needs burning. It was a very stupid thing to do, but I was so full of myself in those days. I imagined myself a female version of Cruikshank or Gillray, famous for my clever wit. I didn't know enough about the world to be witty. David was right, it was little more than smut.'

The anguish in her voice caused his heart to twist painfully. 'We all make mistakes when we are young.' Some mistakes were worse than others.

'I do most heartily thank you for your timely intervention.'

'For all my bragging, I was unable to discover the identity of the man you met in the lane before it was time for you to meet him. He covered his tracks with the cunning of a fox. I was very nearly too late this evening, having gone off on another wild goose chase. Fortunately, when I realised he had slipped my grasp, I knew where to find him and you.'

'Well, it is all over now,' she said. 'And we can continue on with our lives. How is the new governess?'

The coolness in her voice gave him pause. Instead of kissing her, which he had been wanting to do since the moment he walked into her cottage, he followed her lead with the change of topic. Perhaps she needed time to recover from her ordeal.

'She is a very nice young woman. Very well educated.'

'The girls are behaving themselves?' she asked casually, but she must have sensed his reservations.

'Janey is fine, but Elizabeth keeps telling her that she is not doing things the way you did them. She is not co-operating. And she has been up to her old pranks.'

'Oh, dear. I received a letter from Lizzie. She did not mention any problems.'

He looked grim. 'I doubt she sees it as a problem that she put a frog in the woman's bed and has dropped and broken her slate about ten times this week.'

'What about the riding lessons?'

'The pony arrives tomorrow, but she now says she wants nothing to do with it.'

She looked thoughtful. 'I am surprised. What does your governess recommend?'

'Today she suggested leaving her in the nursery with Netty while she teaches Jane on her own.'

'I agree. If she is going to behave like a baby, then she should be treated as one. I must say I am very surprised. She promised me she would give the woman a fair chance.'

He looked grim. 'I gave her a list of rules before the woman arrived. To make my expectations clear, you understand. To ensure it went well.'

She shook her head at him. 'Oh, Jack. Really? You do not think that is a little too much?'

Jack. He liked it that she was calling him Jack again, instead of Lord Compton. If he could not be her lover, then he would very much like to be her friend. Or at least he would accept that was all she had to offer.

'What?' he asked.

Chapter Sixteen

Marguerite didn't really have the right to interfere, but she could feel his unhappiness and confusion. She also felt terrible for Lizzie. His need for rules, for control, was the one thing about him that scared her. She feared a spirited child like Elizabeth might find it too irksome, as she had found it irksome with Neville.

'She is trying to manipulate me,' he continued. 'Saying she will be as good as gold if I make you return. As if I can make you do anything.'

'She is a very clever little girl. She needs a mother, I think.'

He swallowed. 'I know. She wants me to marry you.'

Marriage to Jack. Her heart leapt at the thought. And her stomach sank. She had been subjected to one man's authority, how could she give up her freedom to another? Especially one with a list of rules. 'Good lord! What on earth put that idea in her mind?'

He grimaced ruefully. 'Would it be so very bad?

We are clearly attracted to each other. The girls are so much happier…'

Her heart picked up speed. Something inside her surged with hope and longing. She held her breath, wondering, fearing…

He flexed his hands. 'Of course, I am not suggesting you continue teaching them as you did before you left. Naturally the governess would remain. You don't even have to be involved with them all that much. It would be a comfort to them simply knowing you are there.'

What on earth was he suggesting? 'You mean you are asking me to be a sort of figurehead? To enter into a marriage of convenience?'

He winced. 'I would not put it quite that way. We are compatible, I believe. There is an attraction between us, is there not? I want us to be husband and wife.'

Cold trickled through her veins. A sense of dread. 'And do you also have a list of rules your wife must abide by?'

He hesitated. 'I did think there were a few things…'

As she had thought. He would rule her the way Neville had. Much as she liked him, was attracted to him—perhaps even loved him, because she was some sort of fool—she could never go back to that. 'I am flattered by your offer, but I have lived under the thumb of one husband. I cannot go through that again.'

He stared at her. 'You surely do not compare me to Saxby,' he said, clearly affronted.

'My husband controlled my every waking moment. When I would eat. Who I would see. What I would write in my letters to my family. I will not give over the control of my life to someone else.'

He looked horrified. 'That is certainly not what I intend. I simply have a list of a few common-sense—'

She rose to her feet. 'I like you, Jack. I really do, but if you cannot trust my common sense—'

'Really. And what about this blackmailer chap? Was paying him common sense?'

Anger rose in her breast. 'It might not have been your way of handling the problem, but I did not want to embroil anyone else in my mistake. I am certainly grateful for your assistance, but that does not mean that I would not have been able to deal with him. Eventually.'

She was so angry her breath was coming in short gasps. Not just angry. Disappointed. Hurt.

'My wife died because she did not trust me with her problems. If she had come to me, told me about her brother needing money, instead of sneaking out to meet him in the middle of the night, she would be alive today. Yes, it was bad luck that a criminal had entered our grounds, looking for the main chance, but if she had abided by the rules and not ventured out in the middle of the night, then she would not have been murdered for the few coins she carried. I had not forbidden her to go out. I should have. Why can you not obey a few simple rules designed to keep you safe?'

The pain in his voice was palpable. Clearly, he blamed himself for his wife's death.

'You would have given her brother the money if she had come to you?'

'Of course not. I would have told him to approach his father like a man, instead of preying upon his sister's soft heart.'

'She would have known your feelings on the matter.'

He nodded tersely. 'Yes. I did not have a very high opinion of her brother.'

'Which is why she did what she did. It was her decision. No list of rules wold have prevented her going to meet him.'

He let go a harsh-sounding breath. 'Then how was I supposed to protect her?'

She felt for him, deeply. 'Not by controlling her every movement. All it does is drive a wife to go behind your back. It wasn't your fault or hers that a criminal saw her leave the house and meet her brother. He saw the opportunity and took it. If he had not been there that night, you would have been none the wiser and all three of you would have been happy. After all, he was the intruder. She would have thought herself perfectly safe within the confines of your estate. She is not to blame and you are not to blame. The man who murdered her is the only one at fault.'

He shrugged. 'A husband is supposed to protect his wife.'

'And who do you blame when a criminal comes up before you at the assizes? Do you blame the parents for the acts of a criminal? Do we not all bear responsibility for our own decisions? A woman is just as responsible as a man, surely?'

He sank down on to the chair. 'Her father thought otherwise. He wanted to know why I wasn't taking charge of my family. Of my wife. I vowed then I would make sure I would be in control in future.'

'I expect your father-in-law was looking for someone to blame, other than himself. Did you ever wonder why her brother didn't apply to his father for the money?'

'I know why. He was a spoiled brat. His father had already paid his debts once and said he would not do so again. And that is why—' Jack closed his eyes. 'You are right. I have been blaming myself all this while. The only person to blame is the murderer.'

'Is it possible Lizzie, having become used to the freedoms she has enjoyed recently, found the return to previous rules unfair and she is blaming the new governess?'

He sighed. 'I think you are right about that, too. I did curtail their walks in the afternoon. The thought of them wandering around in the woods with a woman I do not know or trust the way I know and trust you—' He shook his head. 'I could not allow it.' He took a deep breath. 'But I must, must I not?'

'Yes. You must.'

'And about the other matter…my proposal.'

Everything in her heart wanted to say yes. She yearned to accept. Her insides trembled with longing. But how could she marry knowing that as soon as she did, she would lose all her rights to herself, body and soul? How could she trust him to understand she could be trusted without some list of rules by which to order her life? Besides, he needed an heir. She had never wanted children. She wanted her freedom. She shook her head. 'I really like you, Jack. I am attracted to you, but I do not think I am ready for marriage. I am not sure I will ever be ready.'

He gave her a stare full of disappointment. 'So, you expect me to trust my eight-year-old daughter to go exploring without coming to harm, but you will not trust me to be your husband, to honour and cherish you without becoming a tyrant?' A thread of anger ran through his words. She had hurt him.

'I am going to miss you terribly. And the girls, too, but I simply am not ready to give up my freedom and enter into a marriage as a matter of convenience.' She loved him too much for that.

She stilled. She did love him. But that was not what he was offering. And once she was married, could she trust a man who did not love her to keep his word? Confusion filled her mind. She wanted to trust him. But… 'I would prefer us to remain friends, if that is possible?'

He nodded slowly. 'If you ever change your mind…come to me. I'll be waiting.'

The thought of him waiting and hoping was like a

blow to her heart. 'No. Please. Do not wait. I will not change my mind. I like my independence too well.'

He picked up his hat and gloves and bowed. 'Then I bid you goodnight.'

He closed the door softly behind him.

She covered her face with her hands and wept. She should have said yes. She was being a coward. She simply could not pluck up the courage.

'Good morning, Papa.'

Jack lifted his gaze from his paperwork to smile at his eldest daughter as she perched herself on the chair facing him across his desk.

'Good morning, Elizabeth. How are you today?'

Elizabeth had taken it upon herself to report once a week on the affairs of the schoolroom. She had developed some odd notion that she was now the lady of the house. Since their tête-à-tête on his return from his abysmal attempt to woo Lady Marguerite, she had been a model pupil and a happy little girl. Except for the days on which she presented herself in his study. On those occasions she was all business.

'I am fine, Papa.' Her little mouth pursed. 'Actually, I am cross with Janey.'

'Why?'

'She will not listen to me when I tell her it is my turn to ride the rocking horse.'

Miss Ladbrooke had mentioned there were some arguments over the horse. 'Perhaps I should return it to the attic, if it is such a bone of contention.'

She frowned. 'Oh, no. Then no one can have a turn. I just need Janey to listen when I tell her to get off.'

'Perhaps it would be better if you asked her nicely.' He could recall similar arguments with his friends at school. They always resulted in fisticuffs.

Lizzie looked thoughtful. 'Lady Marguerite said if we don't tell each other how we feel, how are we supposed to know? But I cannot tell Janey how I feel if she won't listen.'

Marguerite again. 'Try talking with her about it when you are not in the heat of the moment. When you are not actually arguing about whose turn it is.'

Lizzie tilted her head. She nodded slowly. 'Yes, Papa. I will try. Thank you.'

He smiled at his serious-faced daughter. She was such a pet and so easy to read. 'Was there something else you wanted to discuss.'

She nodded. 'Yes, Papa. Nanny James told Miss Ladbrooke it is time for her to retire. Netty is old enough to begin her lessons and Nanny says since she is no longer needed she would like to go and stay with her sister. She plans to speak to Mrs York about it today.'

'Netty is still a baby,' he said, unwilling to admit the passage of time.

Lizzie stared at him gravely. 'She is nearly three, Papa. I started my lessons when I was three. Nanny said so.'

'Is Miss Ladbrooke willing to take on another pupil, I wonder?' The new governess had settled in really well after a shaky start. He certainly did not want to scare her off by adding another charge to her duties.

'Oh, yes,' Lizzie said airily. 'She is quite consanguine about the idea.'

Consanguine? Oh. He forced himself not to grin. 'You mean sanguine, my dear. Consanguine addresses the closeness of two individuals' relationship to each other.'

She wrinkled her nose. 'I know that. Actually, I thought it was a strange thing for her to say when I looked up the meaning. But you are right, sanguine is what she said.'

He gave her a sharp look and she blushed. 'Well, no. She said the other word. But it must have been what she meant.'

He sighed. He would have to have a word with Miss Ladbrooke about checking the meaning of words before she used them. The woman tried her best, but she was not Lady Marguerite, that was certain. Lady Marguerite would never have made such a mistake.

Although very nice, she was not Lady Marguerite in so many ways.

'Why are you sad, Papa?' Lizzie asked.

He realised with a start he had let his mind wander to the ways in which the governess was nothing like his beloved. Damn. He was trying his best not to think of Marguerite that way. They were friends. Mere acquaintances, now. 'I am not sad, dear. Why do you say that?'

'Because you hardly laugh any more. Not even at Netty's antics.'

Didn't he? He hadn't noticed. 'I am very busy at the moment. Dealing with lambs and planting and such.'

She nodded. 'Can we have a party for Nanny James?'

'A party?'

'Yes. To say goodbye.'

'I expect the servants—'

She stuck out her jaw. 'No. Our family should hold a party. She raised us and Mama, too. She deserves a good send-off. Miss Ladbrooke says her family had a party for her nanny when the old lady retired.'

Good for Miss Ladbrooke. Devil take it, what harm could it do? 'Very well. And who is to be invited to this party?'

'Just family, mostly. Laughton, of course. And Mrs York and all the footmen and Mr Plum the gardener. Lucy. Me and Jane and Netty and you. I will look after the arrangements and the invitations. Miss Ladbrooke says it will be a good exercise for me to learn about my future duties as a wife.'

He stared at her in astonishment. 'Good heavens, child, you are far too young to be thinking of such things.'

Lizzie looked crushed.

'Oh, very well. If Miss Ladbrooke thinks it is a good idea, then I will leave the matter entirely in your hands.'

She cheered instantly. 'Thank you, Papa.' She rose and dipped a little curtsy.

He sat back in his chair and held his arms out. She came around the desk and kissed his cheek while he gave her a hug. 'Run along, poppet,' he said. 'I will see you later for your riding lesson.'

'Yes, Papa. Do not be late, like last time.' She skipped out of the door.

His little girl was growing up.

Perhaps that was why he had felt so weary lately. He was getting old. Was thirty-five old?

'You are invited to attend the farewell party for Nanny James,' the invitation read. The handwriting was childishly rounded and sported a couple of blots where the pen had dripped on to the paper.

The event was an al fresco breakfast beside the lake and set for the next day at two in the afternoon at Bedwell Hall. Only regrets were requested in reply.

There was a postscript on the reverse. 'Nanny James asked for you to come especially.'

Marguerite winced. No doubt Jack would be in attendance and that was going to be terribly embarrassing for both of them. But how could she refuse?

She had told the girls she would be their friend for ever and clearly this farewell to Nanny James was an important event in their young lives. And yet another loss. A friend did not refuse an invitation when clearly their support in trying times was needed.

The idea of having a party for a servant was rather odd, but then, Nanny James was more like family than a servant. Besides, Marguerite missed the girls. Lizzie's letters were far too short to tell her very much about their true state of health and mind. And they never spoke of Jack at all.

She wanted to know that he was all right. That he was happy. She also wanted to assure herself that she had been right to refuse him. Blast it, she wanted to know if they could remain friends. The thought of never seeing him again was painful indeed.

Chapter Seventeen

'Are we holding this party out of doors?' Jack asked Lizzie, observing the activities of his footmen carrying blankets and baskets and chairs across the lawn and beyond the ha-ha.

'Yes. It is al fresco,' Lizzie said, coming to stand beside him.

Jack glanced at the sky. There were a few puffy clouds floating by, but it was as fine a day as one could hope for in the spring. 'Nanny James hates going out of doors. Her rheumatism plagues her if she gets the slightest bit of damp air anywhere near her.'

'She is making an expectation,' Lizzie said.

'Exception.'

'Yes.'

Jack sighed. What he had thought would be a half-hour of tea and cakes in the nursery with the servants standing around looking uncomfortable was turning into a major banquet given the number of baskets of food being paraded across the lawn. 'Exactly where are you holding it?'

'Beside the lake. It has the prettiest view.'

He turned away from the window. 'Well, young lady, I suggest you go and make sure all is in readiness for your guests. I will be there at the appointed time.'

Lizzie shuffled her feet. 'Papa, since you are the host, would you mind coming a half-hour before to be ready to greet our guests, in case anyone comes early?'

'What sort of anyone? It is only us and the servants.'

'It is what the host is supposed to do,' she said stubbornly. She clasped her hands before her in a gesture of appeal. How could any man resist that look in those large brown eyes?

'Very well, I will be there a half-hour before the guests are due to arrive.'

'Thank you, Papa.' She beamed. 'Then you should probably go and dress.'

He shook his head, but could not resist smiling at her happiness. 'Very well, daughter. Off I go to do your bidding.'

They left the study together, but Lizzie headed for the kitchen, while Jack headed upstairs where he found his valet waiting to help him into a coat of blue superfine and a pair of buff pantaloons. 'Do not tell me my daughter decided this is what I should wear to this party of hers.'

'She wants you to look your best, my lord,' his unflappable valet answered, assisting him out of his morning jacket and into something almost fit for a London ballroom.

Perhaps he ought to have a word with Miss Ladbrooke. Lizzie was taking this idea of being the lady of the house too far.

Nevertheless, he arrived at the grassy area beside the lake at exactly two o'clock. Blankets were scattered on the lawn. There were several chairs set beside four small tables, no doubt for those who would not feel comfortable sitting on the grass. There was also a trestle table set beneath a large shady oak tree and the baskets he'd seen earlier were ranged along it.

The lake gleamed in the spring sunshine. The trees on the little island in the middle stirred with the light breeze and the vista from here was spectacular. Lizzie was right, it was the prettiest spot on the Bedwell estate.

'Lord Compton.'

He spun around. A vision in a pale blue gown, a lacy shawl and a little straw bonnet, holding a jaunty yellow sunshade, walked briskly across the lawn.

'Lady Marguerite?' It seemed Lizzie was right. Someone had come early. A faint suspicion leaked into his mind. Was this some sort of plot? 'I had no idea— I mean, welcome. You are a little early, but everyone should be here shortly.'

She looked puzzled. 'Early? My invitation said two.'

What the devil? 'Mine said half-past two, but I was asked to be here a half-hour before.'

They both looked at each other and laughed. 'It seems we are to be given some time alone,' she said. 'Lizzie's idea, do you think?'

The back of his neck prickled. Was Lizzie hiding somewhere? Watching? 'I beg your pardon. If I had any notion of what was planned, I would have warned you.'

'She is quite the rascal,' she said, smiling wistfully. 'I do miss your daughters, you know.'

He missed Marguerite like the very devil. He put out his arm. 'Walk with me, while we wait for the rest of them to show up. Heaven knows what time it says on their invitations. Besides, the view is lovely and the day perfect for a stroll.'

They sauntered down to the lake. There was a punt tied up at the dock. A ribbon fluttered at its prow and the cushion on the seat looked comfortable.

'My word, it is years since I had a boat out,' Jack said.

'It looks inviting.'

And offered a chance to be alone. He'd been thinking about his talk with Lizzie. About how another person couldn't know how you felt if you didn't tell them. He'd not really told Marguerite how he felt. Perhaps this was his chance, when there was nothing else going on and no one to interrupt them.

And if she rejected him again? He was going to feel like an idiot. But at least he would not spend the rest of his life wondering if he should have said what was in his heart.

'Allow me.' He helped her into the punt.

She smiled teasingly. 'Are you sure you know what you are doing?'

He pushed the boat off, leapt in and picked up the pole. 'Let us hope so.'

She laughed. She sounded carefree.

He felt happy. He had felt happy since the moment he turned and saw her walking towards him, as if the sky was bluer and the birds' song was sweeter and the air was warmer.

For the first few minutes, he punted slowly along, following the bank and letting the beauty of the day wash through him.

She twirled her parasol and smiled up at him. 'You are an expert.'

He grinned. 'I am simply praying the pole doesn't get stuck in the mud.'

She laughed. 'How are you, Jack?'

He loved hearing his name on her lips. 'I am well. How are you?'

'Much better now my problems are solved, thank you. I am waiting to hear from my publisher about a new project.'

He turned the craft and headed for the island in the middle of the lake.

She gave him a quizzical glance.

'If I remember correctly, you can see Bedwell Hall from this island. I have often thought it would be a good place from which to paint a view of the house. Perhaps you would care to give me your opinion?'

Her mouth turned down a fraction. 'I am no landscape painter, but if you wish...'

He did wish. He wished for so much more.

They made a gentle landing amid the reeds growing around a small landing stage where they debarked without getting their feet wet.

The island was more overgrown than Jack remembered. He used to come here regularly as a boy, but he had never brought his daughters here. He should have. He would, later this afternoon.

He forced a path through the undergrowth, holding back brambles for Lady Marguerite to pass by until they reached the bank on the other side. From here they could clearly see the picnic area. There were still no other guests in sight. How long had Lizzie given him to be alone with Marguerite?

She came up alongside him and looked out. 'Oh, my word, yes. This would make a wonderful painting.'

He tucked her hand under his arm. 'Would you paint it for me?'

'Oh, Jack. Thank you so much for asking me, but I do not think I could do it justice.'

'How will you know if you do not try? Besides, I have seen your drawings. They would do justice both to nature and the architecture.'

She looked doubtful.

'Think about it,' he said. 'I am confident you can do this, because you care about Bedwell and the family.' He cast her a quick glance. 'Of course, it would require you spending many hours here.'

She made a soft sound of protest. 'You are surely not suggesting we continue our affair?'

Did she have to sound so dismissive?

'No. Actually I am not.'

'Oh, I see.'

Was that a hint of disappointment in her voice? He surely hoped so. He led her to the small wrought-iron bench someone had thoughtfully set here.

He smiled at a recollection. 'When I was a boy, this was the prow of my ship as I sailed up the Amazon or down the Nile.' Today it was a haven of peace with a beautiful view. He seated her and sat down beside her, enjoying the feel of her thigh against his in the tight space.

'You had a vivid imagination as a boy,' she said.

'I did. As an only child it helped pass the time. At least, until my papa decided it was time to learn the business of being an earl.'

'Would you have sooner gone adventuring?'

He thought about that for a moment, as he had not thought about it for years. 'No. I am perfectly content. Or at least almost perfectly content.'

'Almost?'

He took a deep breath. 'I find I enjoy things more when there is someone with whom to share them.'

Her hand shifted beneath his arm, but he pretended not to notice.

'You miss your wife,' she said. 'I expect you will marry again. You need an heir.'

'I would like an heir of my body, but there are cousins and so forth, if I am not fortunate enough to find the right partner.'

'The right partner?'

'My first marriage was arranged by our parents. I came to love my wife, as I love my children. But I was never *in* love. I did not know what that meant.'

He turned. The view of her face was just as lovely as the scenery. Perhaps more so, despite that she looked anxious. He hated the worry on her face, yet if he did not speak, how would she ever know of his feelings?

She opened her mouth to speak, but he pressed a finger to her lips. 'Let me finish, please. I was a fool when I proposed to you.'

She blinked. 'Oh.'

He frowned, but shook off the feeling he had said something wrong. Instead, he charged ahead. 'I should have told you how I have come to care for you. I hope and pray I have not left it too late to do so. While I adore the way my children accepted you into their hearts, I never told you how much *I* love *you*. I love you more than life itself, to be honest. Since you left, I have been surrounded by people, yet I have felt lonely. It was as if a gloom had descended upon me. My children bring me great happiness, but you bring me joy. That is why I wish us to wed. I can only hope I am not too late in speaking of what is in my heart.'

She put her free hand to her breast. 'Jack. I am dreadfully fond of you. I have missed the children terribly. And I have missed you. I—I do love you. Deeply. I am just afraid—'

'If it makes any difference, I must tell you I threw away my lists of rules. I was stupid to think I could control everything and everyone around me. I have come to the conclusion that when two people love each other, they find the right path together.'

He glanced at her troubled expression with trepidation, but continued, since there would likely not be another opportunity to say all that was on his mind. 'I do realise this is rather sudden for you, though I have known these things in my heart for quite some time. If your heart is not engaged the way mine is, I will understand. Whatever your decision, I will respect it and will not press you again after today, though I find it hard to imagine my life without you. Honestly, I could not let you go without telling you how deeply I love you.'

Marguerite had never seen Jack look so hopeful or so anxious, when to her he had always seemed so full of confidence. Her heart seemed to swell in her chest. It took courage for a man to reveal his feelings, but the part of what he said that struck her to the depth of her being was what he had said about his rules. And about partnership.

That was what her sisters had with their husbands, she realised. That was what made them seem so happy and at peace. They were loved, but more importantly they were respected and trusted.

And that was the foundation of love. Mutual trust. In her heart, she knew he was not a man who would ever go back on his word. He was honourable and true and kind and caring. And he loved her.

And she trusted in his love. And, yes, she trusted in hers, too. 'I do love you, Jack.'

'But?'

'But nothing.'

He frowned. 'Are you saying you will marry me?'

She smiled, picked up his gloved hand resting on his knee and brought it to her lips. 'Yes, Jack. I am saying yes.'

He gusted out a sigh, scooped her up and sat her on his lap. He proceeded to kiss her. With passion and desire and...

'Jack,' she muttered. 'The other guests will arrive on that bank over there in a very few moments.'

He lifted his head. 'So... Am I not permitted to kiss my fiancée?'

'Oh, my word. Yes, I suppose you are.'

'Wait. I have something. I meant to do this properly, but I was so worried you were going to say no again—' He retrieved a little velvet bag from his pocket and pulled out a pretty ring of rubies and diamonds. 'This was my grandmother's.' He slid her off his lap and dropped to one knee.

'Marguerite, my darling, will you marry me?'

She couldn't help herself, her smile seemed almost too wide for her face. 'Yes,' she whispered. 'Yes, please.'

She bent forward and kissed his lips.

He pulled her down and held her close, kissing until she could not breathe.

To the sound of applause, they broke apart.

He groaned. There on the bank, across the water, stood everyone who lived and worked at Bedwell Hall.

'Your eldest daughter is looking very pleased with herself,' Marguerite said.

'And so she should. She reminded me of something you said that gave me the courage to do this today—she said you told her, if you do not put your feelings into words how can the other person know what is in your heart.'

'Oh, my, I did say that, did I not? But I can assure you I was not talking about you and me.'

He looked smug. 'No, but I was.'

She gave him a fond smile. 'And you are right.'

He chucked her under the chin. 'No, my dearest darling, we are right.'

She sighed with happiness. 'So we are.'

'Come, let us go back to the party. We have provided enough entertainment for one day.'

She pulled his head down and kissed him hard. When she was done she smiled up at him with a satisfied smile. 'Now we have done enough. Let us go bid farewell to Nanny and announce our news.'

Hand in hand they wandered back to the punt.

Epilogue

The Bedwell Hall music room resounded with happy chatter as the wedding guests followed Marguerite and her now lawfully wedded husband to the dining room, where a wedding breakfast awaited them.

She and Jack had decided to hold the wedding by special licence and invite only family, since they had both been married before and neither of them wanted to wait a moment longer to enter the state of wedded bliss.

At the entrance to the dining room they halted and turned to greet their guests as they passed in.

Her sisters and their husbands were the first to offer their congratulations.

'I am so happy for you, lass,' Carrie said, whose hug was somewhat hampered by a little bulge at her waistline.

'I am delighted you had the courage to travel in your condition,' Marguerite said.

Carrie beamed up at her handsome husband.

Though she was tall for a woman, her husband was taller. 'Avery was a little nervous, but knowing how important my sisters are to me, he put up only a little bit of an argument.'

Avery winked. 'I had the ducal coachmaker adjust the springs and install extra cushions.'

'Let me tell you, I am lucky I did not have to share the coach with a doctor and a midwife,' Carrie grumbled good-naturedly.

'My dear, you wrong me,' Avery said with a twinkle in his eye. 'They have their own coach and followed behind.'

Carrie greeted Jack with a hug and a kiss.

Avery leaned forward and kissed Marguerite on the cheek. 'Congratulations, dear sister-in-law. You picked a fine man. I have never seen you so happy.' He moved on.

She was. Oh, she really was. She glanced at Jack, who was now shaking hands with Avery. He looked so handsome in his wedding clothes.

All the worries she had experienced the day before, the doubts and the fears, had flown out of the window the moment they said their vows. She loved Jack and she knew, without a doubt, that he loved her.

He caught her glance and smiled. Contentment shone from his eyes. Yes, it had taken courage, on both their parts, but they had made the right choice.

'You look lovely, Marguerite,' Petra said. 'And clearly you are deliriously happy. I know, because I am deliriously happy, too.'

She and Ethan had returned from Bath the moment Marguerite had written to tell them the news of her impending marriage. Petra had insisted that Marguerite move in with them for the three days it took to obtain the special licence and had rallied the ladies in Westram village to help make her a wedding gown in a lovely shade of ivory sewn with pearls.

Deliriously happy. Yes, she was. Something she had never expected.

'Congratulations, my dear,' Ethan said and kissed her with military precision on both cheeks, something he must have learned during his time on the Continent.

They, too, moved on and then it was Red's turn. Her brother looked different to the last time she had seen him. As if a great weight had been lifted from his shoulders. 'Red,' she said and he pulled her close and hugged her.

'You picked a good man this time,' he said quietly in her ear.

'I did not pick the last one,' she said. 'Father did.'

'Yes, I know.' He stepped back. 'I warned him against Saxby, but it fell on deaf ears. I'm afraid the man was a bit of a bounder.'

Red did not know the half of it. But it was all in the past and she was so looking forward to her future.

He moved on to shake hands with Jack as she greeted the vicar. 'Thank you for a lovely service,' she said to him.

'My very great pleasure,' said the Reverend Purvis.

Last but not least came her daughters—Lizzie, Janey and Netty—dressed in their prettiest dresses and their faces shining both with the soap and water Lucy must have used to make sure they looked their best and with excitement.

'Mother?' Lizzie said hesitantly.

Marguerite bent and opened her arms to all of them. 'Daughters,' she said and gave each of them a kiss. They walked into the dining room together. The children were to eat with the grown-ups for once and were seated alongside her and Jack.

When everyone had found their places, Red rose to his feet. 'To the happy couple, Marguerite and Jack.'

The guests rose and lifted their glasses. 'Marguerite and Jack.'

'Mother and Father,' Lizzie said and everyone chuckled and resumed their seats.

The sound of happy voices and the chink of cutlery against china filled the room. While the food looked delicious, Marguerite could not eat a bite. Her heart was far too full to have room for anything else.

'Where are you going for your honeymoon?' Carrie asked.

'Bedwell Hall,' she and Jack answered together. Neither of them had wanted to leave the girls right after the wedding, much to their daughters' relief.

'It is a lovely house,' Carrie said. 'The park, what I have seen of it, is beautiful.'

'It is,' Marguerite said.

'The next time you are here, I would be pleased to give you a tour,' Jack said. 'And you are all welcome to visit whenever you wish.'

The butler left his post behind Jack's chair to speak

with a footman who had appeared in the doorway to the kitchens. The butler frowned and shook his head.

The footman handed him a card. Laughton's mouth pursed, then he nodded. He crossed the room and spoke quietly in Jack's ear. 'There is a gentleman here. An officer. He is anxious to speak to Lord Westram. He followed him all the way from Gloucestershire, having missed him there.'

'Westram,' Jack said. 'You have a visitor. Apparently, the matter is urgent. My butler will show you to the drawing room.'

Looking puzzled and slightly worried, Red followed the butler out of the room.

The conversation lulled.

'I am sure it is nothing,' Marguerite said brightly. 'Tell me, Petra, how was your visit to Bath?'

Petra beamed. 'You have never seen such a set of quizzes in your life. And every one of them a friend to Ethan's aunt. The old dear was very happy to see us, and showed us off as if we were royalty.'

Red came back into the room, looking stunned.

'What is it?' Jack said. 'Bad news.'

'I— Not bad news. But it is news my sisters should hear. In private.'

'Whatever it is, I would rather Jack hear it, too,' Marguerite said.

The other sisters agreed with regard to their husbands.

'Laughton, give us the room, please,' Jack said. 'Miss Ladbrooke and Lucy, please take the children to the nursery.'

Lizzie gave him a dark look.

'Lizzie,' Marguerite said. 'If this is something that has import for you and your sisters, I will tell you. I promise.'

After a moment of hesitation, Lizzie dipped a curtsy and left with the others.

Red came to stand beside Jack at the head of the table. 'The officer I met with just now has news of Jonathan, my brother, and his two friends, Harry Davenport and Neville Saxby.'

Marguerite felt the blood rush from her head. Why now? Why did his name have to come up now when she had thought she could at last be happy?

Jack rose and came around behind her, putting his hands on her shoulders, steadying her. She took a deep breath.

Red looked down at the note and then glanced around the table. 'This note was written by my brother shortly before he was killed. It was found in the pocket of his coat which had been stolen from him by a French soldier after his death. It surfaced when the man was captured recently.' He took a deep breath. 'Jonathan was my brother and while he made some mistakes, he had sworn to do better and I believed him. It was why I encouraged his marriage to Carrie. Honestly, I never understood why he left right after the ceremony.' He turned to look at Carrie and then at Marguerite. 'Apparently, he and Harry were on their way into the church when he saw Neville strike Marguerite.'

Marguerite gasped. She remembered. She'd been

late because she'd torn a flounce on her gown and he'd been furious. He'd punched her in the middle of her back as she had got out of the coach. He had been very good at leaving bruises where they wouldn't be seen.

Red's hand shook as he glanced down at the paper. He looked up at his sister. 'Harry told Jonathan it wasn't the first time he'd seen Neville strike you.' His face was full of pain. 'You should have told me.'

Marguerite felt the blood drain from her face. 'What could you have done?'

Red's lips went white. 'I would have done something. Anyway, Jonathan went for Neville's throat right after the ceremony and the coward ran off. Jonathan could not let it go. He went in pursuit. Harry went after Jonathan, to help bring the scoundrel back and to prevent Jonathan from committing murder. To cut a long story short, Harry and Jonathan followed Neville all the way to the battle front, intending to have it out with him. Jonathan wrote this note in Dover, explaining his departure, but for some reason, never posted it.'

Carrie put a hand to her throat. 'I thought he ran off because he never wanted to marry me in the first place.'

'Apparently, the man wasn't such a fool after all,' Avery said drily.

'Well, I have to say I resented him a good deal at the time,' Carrie said. 'But it resulted in great happiness for me.'

'And me,' Petra said, giving her husband a speaking glance. 'Chasing after Jonathan without a word to anyone was just the sort of thing Harry would do. He never gave a thought for anyone but his friends.'

'If anyone was to blame, it is Neville,' Marguerite said. 'He was an awful man.'

Jack put an arm around her waist and brought her to her feet. He held her close and she felt protected and safe.

That was who Jack was. A man who protected those he loved.

Avery pulled Carrie close and Ethan put an arm around Petra's shoulders.

They all looked at Red, who looked devastated. He straightened his shoulders. 'Perhaps if I had seen what was happening to Marguerite, their deaths might have been avoided. But I did not.' He looked at his sisters, his eyes full of anguish. 'I see you are happy. I am happy for you, I truly am, but I think I need some time alone.'

'Red,' Marguerite said, knowing her brother only too well. 'Please. Do not blame yourself.'

He looked at her starkly. 'If not me, then who?'

He left before anyone could speak.

'He'll come around,' Avery said. 'He needs time. Meanwhile, this is a happy occasion and we will not allow the past to spoil it.'

Marguerite looked at Jack. 'The past cannot spoil the joy of the present.'

'A toast,' Ethan said. 'To the future.'

The six of them formed a circle and put their arms around each other. 'The future.'

'And happiness for all,' Marguerite said.

'Happiness for all,' they said in unison.

'Including Red,' Petra said softly.

The group broke apart and Ethan's carriage was called for. Carrie and Avery were to stay with Petra and Ethan overnight. Jack and Marguerite waved them off.

Finally alone with his wife in his bedroom, Jack held her close and kissed her deeply. 'Happy, Wife?' he asked when they finally broke apart.

'I have never been happier in my life,' Marguerite answered and the joy in her eyes was a pleasure to behold. 'I feel as if I have been given the chance to start my life anew. It is not many people who are so fortunate.'

'I know. I am the luckiest man alive to have won you for my wife,' he said, his heart so full, it felt as if it might actually be too large for his chest.

She glanced at the bed. 'I know it is early, my darling, but do you think there might be time...?'

He grinned like a naughty boy. 'I think we might have all the time in the world, my dearest Marguerite.'

She smiled as he pulled her close and nuzzled against her throat.

* * * * *

*If you enjoyed this story,
check out the other books in
The Widows of Westram miniseries:*

**A Lord for the Wallflower Widow
An Earl for the Shy Widow**

*And why not check out these other
great reads by Ann Lethbridge?*

**An Innocent Maid for the Duke
Rescued by the Earl's Vows**